abandoned

abandoned

benjie willow the orphan series
book one

Ash Lingam

WISE WOLF
BOOKS

WISE WOLF BOOKS
An Imprint of Wolfpack Publishing
wisewolfbooks.com
1707 E. Diana Street
Tampa, FL 33610

Paperback ISBN 978-1-965596-09-8
eBook ISBN 978-1-965596-08-1

Benji Willow is dedicated to my favorite Western writer, Larry McMurtry. RIP.

Tread lightly on the earth as there might be thorns.

Choctaw Proverb

abandoned

one
fourteenth birthday

"Can we have the cake before we start our chores, Ma? By the time we get home, it'll be the end of the day and nearly dark. We'll be too tired to eat."

"You boys, too tired to eat?" Mary Willow asked, smiling. "You and your brother are always hungry, Benji."

"Come on, Ma," James said. "It's my birthday, too. I agree with Benji. Plus, it's chocolate cake. I don't see why we should have to wait."

"It'll give us lots of energy, too, Ma." That cake smelled so good I believed I could eat the whole thing. "It'll be cold by the time we get back anyway. Right now, I can see steam rolling off the top. It'll be better fresh from the oven, warm and moist. We ain't had a cake since last year."

My mouth began to water. I smelled the air and smacked my lips. My stomach growled so loud my mom stared. Ma was just starting with the icing as she squeezed it out of a funneled cloth. She slapped my hand with a wooden spoon when I reached out to sneak a taste.

"Ouch!"

"All right then. We'll have it this morning, but you better tell your pa before he rides off." Mary smiled. "If not, we won't see him again until supper, and you'll both have to wait."

"I'll get him." I jumped up and ran for the stables. "Pa! Don't leave yet! Ma said we could celebrate our birthday early today. We're going to have cake for breakfast." I couldn't stop laughing.

"Who came up with such a foolish plan, anyway?" John Willow smiled. "You two could talk your mother into climbing Mount Everest."

"Mount what?"

"Never mind; tell your ma I'll be right there," John said. "You better have a hot cup of coffee waiting for me, young man. Fourteen years old is it already? My, how time flies. You make me feel like an old man, son."

"Once you get a taste of that chocolate cake, you'll forget about being old." I turned and ran to the house, laughing loudly. "I'll get your coffee, Pa. Three spoons of sugar, just how you like it."

John was just strapping on his Colt Walker revolver, which he had brought home with him from the war. He never went to the river unless he was armed, and today, he planned to ride the length of his land. Sometimes, he'd seen Indians crossing from the south bank, but they never bothered us, so we left them alone. He leaned his Winchester rifle against the wall beside the pitchfork.

He kept the information about the Comanche to himself so he wouldn't scare the missus. John believed that surviving the war on the winning side was a sign that his future would be bright, and he had two hard-working boys to help him. In only four years, they had built a fine little ranch.

Don't let your pride fuss with your mind, John Willow, he scolded himself. *A humble man is closest to God.*

"He's coming, Ma!" I was running so fast I slid to a stop and landed on my bottom. James laughed so hard that he got a stitch.

"Go fetch a fresh bucket of water, Benji, while James brings the coffee kettle out. We can eat out here this morning before it gets hot."

"Pa wants another cup of coffee."

"I'll bring the sugar," James said.

"Don't you boys dare do like your father, or your teeth are gonna rot," Mary scolded, but she couldn't hide her smile. Her boys were nearly men.

"What happened to the time? It seems like yesterday I had two little babies to care for. Now you've both gone and grown up on me. Lucky for me, I have a couple of years before you run off, Benji."

"Why would I run off, Ma? I'd never leave you and Pa alone."

"All young men leave at some time or other," Mary said. "It's just the way life is. And you, unlike your brother, are a wonderer. I knew it from when you were ten years old. You were as curious as a cat about what was out in the world. It must be hard to have such a spirit harnessed to a ranch."

"I'll go get that bucket of water. I could use a nice cold drink."

I really didn't know what Ma was talking about, but women were a mystery to me. It had been four years since we had seen another female besides our mother. I wondered if they were all like her.

The well was on the other side of the corral. The first one we dug dried up two years ago, and we had to dig a new one. Lucky for us, Pa knew one of a distant neighbor who was skilled at water dowsing. Pa said the forked stick he used was called a divining rod. Sure enough, he found water.

I talked to the diviner once he was done, and he said all he did was travel, finding water for ranches and farms. He told me it took him all over the country, and it paid well. I thought about it, but I figured it was something that you couldn't learn but had to be born with. I stopped for a moment as I daydreamed about what I might be when I'm grown up. Then I remembered the water.

The wooden bucket sat on top of the round stone water well, and a rope looped through two holes on the sides and strung through the pulley on a twenty-five-foot stretch of rope. When Pa did a job, he did it right. He even lined the inside walls with stones so it wouldn't cave in. The water must have come from a deep spring because it was as cool as watermelon in the early morning, even in the middle of summer.

The sun stood just over the horizon and seemed so

big it dwarfed the countryside. It glowed red along the surface of the Red River. It was the dawn of a new day and a new year of life for some, like me. I reckon soon I could call myself a man. Of the twins, I'm the elder by seven minutes.

That's what I told James, anyway. He was always so easy-going that he was fine with that. I wish I were so carefree. Even though we look exactly alike, we couldn't be more different. Strangely enough, that was something that only James and I knew. Twins had secrets like that. We had a special connection where sometimes I knew what he was thinking, just like he knew what I felt.

When the Comanche came, there was no warning. The only thing that saved me was I was standing beside the well. Luckily, I had the mind to grab the bucket, drop it into the water, and hold on to the rope for dear life. I remember the hemp spun through the pully, making it squeal. I was sure the Comanche would hear it.

It unwound until it hit bottom with a splash and jerked to a stop. My pa had knotted the other end on a small roof post covering the well, intended to keep out debris. With the constant wind, dirt flew like large brown clouds as it raced across the dry land.

Once all the yelling and screaming stopped, I continued to sit on the bucket, swaying just under the water's surface. I stared up wide-eyed for so long that my neck ached, waiting for painted faces to look over the edge and down. In the end, I guess nobody saw me escape. The Comanche were on a killing frenzy and only saw the spoils before them. A half dozen warriors hit our home just after first light, catching us all off guard.

Time passed—I listened until the last hoof-clop died in the distance.

Still, I didn't dare move. My heart hammered between my ears like a bass drum. It felt like it was just about to pop out of my chest. Finally, after hours, I pulled my way to the top and peered over the edge of the stone wall.

I jerked as I suddenly remembered Mother's screams—by the sound of things, she was the last to die. I reckon she suffered more than James and Pa. It sounded like the warriors had passed her around, abusing her before taking her life, too. I knew if they found me, I would follow a fate equal to that of my brother. I squeezed my eyes shut as tight as I could and tried to block out the horrible cries from those I loved and the war cries from the cruelest people on the Plains.

When I climbed out, I glanced at the sun: it said twelve noon. I'd been down there for a long time—over three hours. That's why my legs were numb and my teeth chattered.

When I finally thought it was safe to move around, I walked to the stables and got a pick and shovel. I was going to have to bury Ma, Pa, and James. I tried to fight back the tears, but they rolled down my face anyway. They tasted salty on my lips. A shudder racked me, seeming to last forever.

I tilted my head toward the orange globe, and it warmed my face. Behind me stood the burned-out ruins of my family's ranch house. Scattered across the dirt were my mother, father, and James, my twin brother.

All three were full of arrows. Coagulated blood pooled under their bodies. I had to turn my eyes away so I wouldn't see too much. The harsh Texas sun was already drying up the puddles. Signs of the Comanche war party were everywhere.

I looked around hard, but it was apparent the hostile Indians were gone. I had heard their ponies' hooves clapping away, but still, I thought maybe it was a trick. One or two may have stayed back and were waiting for me in the shadows. I guess I disappeared down the well faster than I thought.

Behind me was a table with four chairs. Our birthday cake lay broken into pieces on the ground. Beside it was my twin. Today, we turned fourteen and were all ready for a party. Now, it no longer mattered how old I was. I doubt I'd live long on my own anyway. The fancy paper hats my mother made tumbled in the wind and floated away along with all my good memories. There was no one left but me. I looked around the ranch house suspiciously. I had to grit my teeth to keep them from chattering. The water in the well was cold.

"I better get the shovel." I wiped a tear from my eye. "I'm fourteen, so I'm now a man whether I like it or not."

I knew I had to do it. I walked over to my father, trying not to look at his head. He got scalped like Mom and James. Red, bare skulls looked bright in the sunlight. Trying not to look, I grabbed his father's old

Colt Walker and gun belt. When I picked it up, the weight surprised me. Till then, he had never let me touch anything but his Winchester rifle, which he taught me how to use. He brought the pistol and rifle home from the war. When I drew back the hammer, it clicked loudly.

Violence was nothing new to those living in Northern Texas near the Red River. This was the home of the feared Comanche Indians, and just over the river were the Indian Territories. Yet, it seemed the Willows were oblivious to the danger. For four years, nobody had bothered them, so they expected no trouble. They had mistakenly staked out a plot on somebody else's land.

They had lost neighbors in the past because they were scared and ran off but not butchered. My father held on to his ranch until the end because it was the only thing he had ever owned. He believed if more White men and their families moved to the area, the Indians would get pushed farther away, but little by little, the surrounding ranches succumbed to the violence perpetrated by the warrior tribe. Finally, only a half dozen ranches were still untouched, but those were to fall soon, too. Nobody would go unscathed.

"After what I saw today, I bet with time, all the ranches will vanish soon enough."

I couldn't help talking to my brother, even though I knew he was dead. Maybe since we're twins, a little bit of him still lived on in me. I could swear I could feel him in there, next to my heart.

It was a hot job digging three graves, but I was

thankful for something to do. It kept me from seeing everything repeatedly in my mind's eye. I knew that as soon as I was done, I would have to leave. It would be too dangerous on the ranch now, and I wouldn't want to stay anyway. There was nothing left for me here.

I had no idea where I would go, but I guessed I would worry about that when I got that far. First, I had to finish burying my kin six feet under. This was the hardest thing I'd ever had to do. My heart felt the weight of a ton of bricks.

I returned to the well to wash off the dirt when I finished. I dipped the ladle into the bucket and greedily slurped the refreshing liquid. That was when I heard the horses. They sounded like shod hooves, but I knew I'd better hide again. I slipped back over the wall of the well, using the bucket to lower myself down again, just far enough so I could peek over the top if I felt it was safe enough. That was when I saw the long pencil-like shadows of two silhouettes of men and horses. I wondered if they were coming to kill me, too.

two
malvo tanner

When Malvo pulled his horse to a stop and looked north, he saw black smoke rising into the sky. He pulled on his long beard and pondered. A cloud of dust followed riders racing from the fire, heading west. He removed his hat, wiped his brow with his sleeve, and slipped it on again, frowning.

"I reckon the Comanche have been at another one of the ranches," Malvo said, but when he looked around, his Choctaw friend was nowhere to be seen. "Now, where did Chito-Ochi run off to again? I swear that man disappears more than most horses pass wind."

As he got closer, his mount nervously shifted his feet, stretched his neck, and pulled at the bit. With eyes like saucers, the horses' noses flared at the smell of blood. He wrapped the lead of the second horse around his fist as the paint struggled to pull himself free.

"Come on, you fool horse," Malvo spat. "Settle down, and let's just try not to make a straight line crooked. All I need is to mess up with Comanche around."

The ex-soldier slowly nudged his animal forward. He drew an 1851 Navy Colt as he reined to a stop. He cocked his head and listened, but all he could hear were blowflies. The smell of death was strong in the air. He noticed three fresh graves at the end of the yard. Closer were drying pools of blood.

That means somebody survived, Malvo thought.

"You can come on out now!" Malvo shouted. "I ain't gonna bite. As you can see, I'm a White man, not a Comanche. I know those folks didn't bury themselves. Lookee here, I'll even put my gun away. Now, don't shoot. I'm friendly."

The youngster was drenched when he clawed out of the stone water well. He stared at the stranger wild-eyed as his teeth chattered.

"W-w-who are you?"

"Why, I'm Malvo Tanner. And I reckon you be kin to the folks under them graves." He nodded, frowning. "You're a mite young to be left alone like that, ain't cha?"

"I-I'm fourteen, Mr. Tanner. The Comanche killed my ma, pa, and brother. I was lucky and hid in the well."

"Well, good for you, boy," Malvo said, forcing small curls onto the edges of his lips.

"This morning, my pa said James and I would be men today, on our birthday. He was my twin brother."

"Twin, ya say," Tanner pondered. "And your birthday, to boot. What a bad streak of luck. Whatcha gonna do now?"

To be honest, the question shocked me. I hadn't thought that far. Getting away with my life seemed to be more than enough for me to absorb—that and losing my family. They even burned the house and most of my things in it.

"I reckon I'll go out and look for one of our horses. Two or three always slip by us when we round up the strays. Then I'll bring them back here and pack what I can find that's not ruined or burned."

When I looked hard at the stranger, he seemed nervous. That was when I remembered the old revolver in my hand.

"Whatcha gonna do with that cannon, young man?" Malvo asked, frowning. "I see you've had a hard time. How did you survive, son? How about puttin' that gun down?"

"I got lucky, and nobody looked in the well." I dropped the gun by my side but didn't un-cock it, just in case. I wasn't ready to completely trust anybody yet.

"I'd say you got away by the skin of your teeth," Malvo said. "The place is riddled with arrows. That stone well saved your bacon, boy. Lucky for you, they didn't get thirsty. I figure you getting away was what they call a miracle."

That was when I saw an Indian riding our way and pointed the heavy revolver right at him. The hammer remained cocked. It was a wonder it didn't go off in my shaking hands. I've never shot anybody before, but I guess there's a first time for everything.

"Stop right there, or I'll shoot!"

"That ain't no Comanche, boy," Malvo said, surprised. "That's a Choctaw Indian from the South Coast back East. He's my partner."

"Your partner? Who has hostile Indians for partners?"

"Well, I reckon I do, for starters, and all Indians aren't hostile. The Choctaw are first-class traders." Malvo turned toward the Indian. "And where in dickens did you run off to again? Every time I turn around, you disappear."

The Indian held up four rabbits. "I brought dinner. What happened here?"

"This here be Chito-Ochi," Malvo said. "I, er, didn't get your name, young man."

"My name's Benji Willow. This is—was the Willow Ranch."

"Pleased to meet cha." Malvo smiled as his Indian friend nodded. "Don't mind him. He takes a spell to side up to strangers, especially if they're White. Even then, he ain't much of a talker."

"We shouldn't stay here," Chito-Ochi warned as he looked around. "There are Comanche pony tracks all over. How many warrior braves came here, Benji?"

"There were six of them, sir."

Chito-Ochi laughed, his eyes full of mischief. His White friend joined in, chuckling.

"What did I say that's so funny?"

"He's just never been called a *sir*." Malvo snickered. "You can call him Chito-Ochi and me Malvo, and we'll get on just fine, Benji. Friends should be on a first-name basis."

"Are we friends now?" Things were moving too fast, and I was confused. How could a man I had just met claim we were friends?

"You better hope so, young man," Malvo said. "If not, you'd be in a world of trouble. Now, let's go look for those horses. Chito-Ochi here is one heck of a tracker. He'll find whatever's out there and keep us out of trouble while doing it."

"What about my saddle? The Comanche didn't burn the stables."

"Well, then, you might as well saddle up one of our spares," Malvo said a little begrudgingly. "We never travel with only one horse. It's too hard on the animals, and you never know when one will come up lame. Losing your horse in the wrong place could cost you your life."

Ten minutes later, the three of them rode toward the river in a dusty wake. Another ten minutes into the ride, the Choctaw Indian disappeared. Malvo swore under his breath.

"Don't mind him," Malvo said. "He does it all the time. I've known Chito-Ochi since before the Civil War, and I can't get him to follow a word I say, so I doubt you will, either. Most Indians do what they want. They're too used to livin' *free*. The Southern Army used Choctaw Indians as scouts."

"All Americans are free. That's what my pa said. That's what he fought in the war for—freedom."

"And on what side was that, Benji?" Malvo asked.

"He fought for the North, sir."

"Well, Benji, my boy, there's free, and then there's free. It all depends on how you look at it. For me, the only free people in this country are the Indians—at least the ones we haven't rounded up and put on reservations. I reckon that was what ticked off the politicians back in Washington so much. They couldn't stand to see a people living so freely."

"I never looked at it that way," I answered, but I still didn't understand.

I wonder if he held it against me for being a Yankee. He didn't seem to flinch when I told him Pa fought for the North. The war had only been over for four years, but the scars still ran deep.

Despite Malvo's looks, he seemed like a decent enough man, but I didn't plan on riding with an Indian after what happened to my family. The first chance I got, I would head off alone. Where would I go? I had no idea. All I knew was that for now, Malvo and his Choctaw friend were my means to escape the Red River. I already knew I would never escape what I saw that day. It was burned into my mind, and it would haunt me for the rest of my life.

It *was* amazing how Chito-Ochi found two horses in a few hours. He even claimed there was another one out there somewhere, but I didn't need two if I wanted to do as Malvo said. Even though I didn't completely trust him, maybe I could learn a thing or two. As a greenhorn traveler, I needed all the help I could get while trying to stay out of trouble. I'd have to watch the Indian like a hawk, or I might wake up without a scalp.

"So, now that you've got your horse, you can ride with us if you want," Malvo offered. "Have you traveled much before, Benji? This isn't the kind of country to ride if you don't know how to take care of yourself."

"I came down the Chisholm Trail with my family, but I was only eleven, so I didn't do much more than tend to the wagon and the livestock. We brought horses with us to breed with the wild ones. My pa was a first-notch rancher. I guess all that doesn't matter anymore, does it?"

"The only thing that matters is that you're still alive, Benji. You should be thankful you're not back there with your brother; God rest his soul. You might be the luckiest man I've ever known or ever will know. People die; that's a fact. Death gets us all in the end. But now you must rejoice in the fact that you're still alive, boy. Miracles don't come but once in a lifetime, if ever."

"I reckon you're right. To tell the truth, it's hard to see past the horror. Every time I close my eyes, I see my parents and my twin brother lying there scalped. Seeing James was like seeing myself dead. I don't know how to describe the feeling. We were identical twins, you know."

"Come on, let's get going, or we're never gonna get to Texas," Malvo said as he gigged his horse and raced off.

Did I understand him to say Texas? I didn't think I misunderstood. I've heard of the place but never thought about going somewhere so far away. I read it was all the way down by the Gulf of Mexico. I couldn't imagine any place so far away, yet my family came across the West from Illinois. That, too, was far. I wonder if that was where I should go next or would there be nothing for me there, either.

I know I don't want to go back East. All I have is crabby old aunts and a couple of ancient uncles who might be dead by now. No, I must strike out on my own and make my own way. Exactly how I will do that remains to be seen; I still have no choice in the matter. It's do-or-die, at this point. I never expected my life to experience such a significant, unexpected change. I never dreamed I'd lose my brother.

three
the territories

Chito-Ochi crept into camp late that night without making a sound. He seemed to walk right out of the shadows. We were just about to turn in after the longest day of my life. Despite the introduction earlier, a sudden anxiousness came over me when the Choctaw scout emerged from the dark.

All Indians seemed alike to me after the Comanche raid. I didn't know if I could sleep at night knowing he was lying on the other side of Malvo. I checked his belt for scalps—I didn't see any, but I saw a big Bowie knife. I imagined it was as sharp as a razor.

Malvo didn't seem surprised by the Indian's mysterious behavior. They were as strange a pair as I had ever met. Yet, something about Mr. Tanner gave me the impression of an honest person, despite his appearance. His brace of pistols and belt looked worn and well-used. His gray eyes were like hardened steel.

He carried Sharps and Winchester rifles in sheaths under the saddle's fender. Of course, he was a Confederate in the war—that much I gleaned from what he said. Still, he didn't seem to hold a grudge against me, despite my father fighting for the North.

That night, I stared silently into the flames, lost in my grief-stricken world. Orange coals reflected in my eyes as cinders ran downwind, disappearing twenty feet from the fire. I looked up and saw millions of stars pulsating like fireflies. Everything looked different to me. After the death of my family, everything felt different, too.

A half-hour later, I heard the men snoring softly, but I couldn't bring myself to close my eyes. Every time I did, I saw James lying on the ground with no hair. I slipped my revolver and holster beneath my saddle so I could get to it quickly if needed. Sweat ran off my brow as I stared blindly into the night. I blinked as the salt burned my eyes.

Crows cawed in the trees overhead, pulling me from an uneasy sleep. Burning wood assaulted my senses, making me wiggle my freckled nose. For a moment, I was back at the ranch as a black cloud covered the sky. When I opened my eyes, I saw Chito-Ochi cooking frying pan biscuits. It was daylight. My mouth began to water. For a moment, I forgot how I got there—even who I was. All I could think about was my hungry belly.

Pushing myself up and onto my elbows, I blinked. "Is there enough breakfast to go around?" I sat up and rubbed the sleep from my eyes with the heels of my hands.

The Choctaw Indian nodded without a word.

Then I heard a noise behind me. I swung around, reaching under my saddle, but my pistol was gone.

"Are ya looking for this?" Malvo asked as the gun belt swung from his hand. "Here ya go, young man." He tossed it on my bedroll. "I didn't want to take a chance that you'd wake up and forget who we were and shoot us with that old cannon. It must weigh five pounds, loaded."

I grabbed my gun a little more quickly than I should have, but I still wasn't sure who I was riding with. But I was alive, and it appeared the Southerner and the Indian didn't intend me harm. I touched the top of my head; I still had my hair.

"Don't you want this?" Chito-Ochi asked as he grabbed a Winchester from his bedroll. "I found it in the stables. I reckon the Comanche were too distracted to give the barn a good search. It leaned beside a pitch-fork in the shadows. Was this your father's?"

I hadn't checked for the rifle when I looked through the stables. It must have been in the far corner hidden in the dark. Then again, I was still in shock and was as confused as I'd ever been.

"Thank you kindly, Chito-Ochi. Yeah, it was my pa's. I plumb forgot. I wonder why the Comanche didn't steal it."

"I reckon they were too pumped up and busy with your folks," Malvo said sadly.

"Sometimes Indian warriors go into a frenzy," Chito-Ochi said. "Maybe they were hopped up on peyote or drunk. Indians and liquor do not mix well."

"You best put all that behind you now, son," Malvo

said. "It's time you forgot about death and got on with living your life. Nothing's going to bring back what once was. This country is unforgiving, so you better get your head around what happened and focus if *you* want to stay alive."

The Indian looked at me curiously and nodded as he passed the hot cast-iron skillet so I could grab a biscuit. It was so hot it burned my fingers, but I didn't mind. I felt like I was starving.

"Ouch!" I cried out when I popped the hot bread into my mouth. It burned my tongue, but I was too hungry to wait.

"Here, put a peach on your biscuit." Malvo chuckled as he stabbed a piece of canned fruit with a knife. "Chito-Ochi is a pretty good cook when it comes to breakfast. I always make supper. I've got more imagination than bacon and eggs."

I forgot my manners and greedily accepted the peach, gobbling it down. I didn't even wait to put it on the biscuit.

"I reckon there's nothing like the hunger of a healthy young man." Malvo chuckled again as he passed me another.

We rode without stopping that day, following the Red River upstream and west. Off and on throughout the day, the Choctaw vanished several times, only to return just as mysteriously as he had disappeared. I didn't think I'd ever understand Indians. Lucky for me, he hadn't presented a threat.

When we saw twelve heavily armed Comanche crossing the Red River from the south bank, we quickly dismounted and pulled our horses into the heavy vegetation growing at the water's edge.

"We better make sure we don't run into the war party," Malvo whispered. "We won't stand a chance against a dozen Comanche. We will have to outsmart them."

"We better swim to the north bank so we can swing wide," Chito-Ochi whispered as he parted the leaves and branches to have a careful look. "If we run into them, it will mean a fight, and I doubt we will win. It should be safer on the other side for now. Later, we will have to see. We must be careful. There are more than Comanche north of the river. That's where many tribes live, including the Cheyenne."

I felt like we were going from a boiling pot to a frying pan, when a couple of days ago, everything was so peaceful. I briefly wondered what the chocolate cake would have tasted like. We had only had chocolate once before since it was so expensive.

Malvo and Chito-Ochi wrenched their horses about and booted them into the stream. As it got deeper, we swam them to the other side, pushing water aside as we went. Men and animals alike drank deeply. As we forded the fast-flowing river, the six horses picked their way over rocks. The water reached our necks as we swam across. I held onto the saddle horn and let my paint pull me, but the current dragged us downstream.

Before I knew it, Chito-Ochi grabbed my reins and led the way when I was about to lose control. Although it only took minutes, it seemed like an hour. I spat up water and then swallowed some more, nearly drowning. Somehow, we ended up safely on the other side, gasping for air as we lay on the far bank. My heart hammered between my temples.

"The Comanche war party will be looking for ranchers to raid on the south side of the river," Chito-Ochi said. "We better head west for a day, then cross back over at night. Tonight, we'll have enough moon to make the cross."

"And the ranchers on the north side?"

"Only red men dare to make their homes north of the Red River," the Choctaw said. "We're in the Indian Territories now. Indian agents are supposed to keep the peace here, but I'm afraid it's too little and nearly always too late."

Malvo uncinched the saddle and pulled it down, hobbling his horse's rear leg to its foreleg. His horse pulled at tufts of grass and slid its jaws.

"You best both do the same. We don't want the horses to wander off if the Comanche show up again. We can rest here for a few minutes—maybe an hour or so, but we've got to get out of sight first," Malvo said as he eyed the southern bank of the river warily. "This country's hard on people—especially families, but I don't have to tell ya that. You've done seen for yourself. I believe it's best to travel alone or with a professional scout like Chito-Ochi. Then, the only thing you've got to lose is your *own* life. Ya know, only fools try to steal land from the Comanche—no offense, son, but you saw what happened to your folks."

"So why did they let us stay for four years? Why

didn't they run us off as soon as we arrived? We could have headed farther south and would have caught up with the wagon train."

"Could have and would have don't mean much out here, Benji. Yeah, I meant to get to the wagon train," Malvo said. "It looks like it could be the same one some ten miles south of here, your pa's ranch. Or at least what's left of it after the attack and with so many years having passed. But there were still wagon wheel rims and human bones scattered about. It could have been the bunch you all came down the Chisholm Trail with. Did you know it's over twenty miles wide?"

"Several wagon trains can pass simultaneously and never see each other," Chito-Ochi said. "But the one due south of your ranch looked like it was on an identical path. Movement has slowed lately due to the Comanche uprising. Any wagons out there now are fair game."

I looked all around us as paranoia grasped me like a vise, making it hard to breathe. I never wanted to see a Comanche again, but that was looking more and more unlikely.

"Maybe the Comanche were thinking about it, waiting for some sign," Chito-Ochi said. "Or to see if your family left on their own. It's hard to get into a Comanche's head, though. They are not like the rest of the Indians."

"Lucky for me, you don't seem to be at all like them. At first, though, I wasn't so sure."

"With time, you will learn that you cannot stop what is coming no matter what you do," Chito-Ochi said. "All things were written in time long before we arrived here and will remain so after we are gone."

The sun sprayed orange rays of light. It fell through the leaves like rain as I wondered what the Choctaw was talking about. Streaks of sun warmed my face. Everything came to me in riddles. My pa used to use a fancy word: conundrum. I reckon that's what this was. I couldn't find another name for it. I suddenly found myself without direction for the first time in my young life. Maybe Chito-Ochi was right. Who knows, perhaps all things *were* meant to be.

After riding all day, darkness seemed to envelop us like a blanket. Lightning bugs lit up one place only to flash seconds later in another. Bullfrogs croaked on the riverbank as coyotes sang their choir in the distance. The musky smell of humidity made the air thick and sticky. I could hear the water lapping against the bank as the current flowed eastward.

"My pa told me the Red River was the second largest river basin in the southern Great Plains. That and it's full of quicksand."

"That is a fact, but Chito-Ochi guides us around such dangers," Malvo said, smiling. "Regarding how big it is, that's news to me. Your pa seemed to be a studied man."

"Nah, not really. He just read a lot—everything he got his hands on, no matter what the subject. Our ma is school-taught—er, she was. She taught James and me to read, write, and do our numbers. The Willow family has been poor for as long as my parents could remember, but my pa was determined to be the first one to have a prosperous ranch."

"One man's riches are another man's rags." Malvo smiled. "Just like one man's gold is trash to another. Being rich ain't always about who has the most money. There are other ways of being wealthy. Why, sometimes I feel like the richest man in the world when others would say I'm a bum, drifting from one place to another with no clear direction. Chito-Ochi and I have been doin' the same since the end of the war. I reckon we didn't have any place to go, either. Pretty much like you. Maybe that's why I couldn't leave ya behind."

"To be honest, at first, I didn't know if I could trust you, especially when Chito-Ochi showed up. In just two days, I feel pleased that you both helped me like you did. I would have probably perished. I thank ya kindly, gentlemen."

"Lookee here, Chito-Ochi." Malvo chuckled. "He's polite and all. And now you've gone from a 'sir' to a gentleman."

The Choctaw Indian laughed so hard he got a stitch, and tears ran down his red cheeks. He smiled, showing a mouth full of white teeth.

four
run for cover

That night, we crossed the river once the moon came up, but we didn't see any more Comanche. When we reached the south bank again, we found a stand of trees where our fire would be hard to see and made camp for the rest of the night. Somehow, crossing in the dark was half as scary. I guess because I could only see a few yards before me. I think there will be more to cross in the future, even though I had no idea where I was going. The glowing globe hung in the sky like it was on a string. It bathed the countryside in a silvery glow.

After tending to the horses and fetching water, we settled in for a long-needed rest. Malvo stood and mumbled something to Chito-Ochi and walked into the night. I immediately wondered if he would return. It had only been days, but I was already attached to the two unlikely characters I traveled with. On a map, I wasn't exactly sure where we were, but we still weren't far from home.

When we were alone while Malvo went out to do his business, Chito-Ochi said, "Sometimes Tanner troubles me like a woman. I think his mother mated with a scorpion. Mind you, he ain't as mean as he looks."

The Indian looked at me from the corner of his eye to see my reaction. I didn't know if he was baiting me or what.

"What makes you say such a thing? I feel more comfortable with him than I do with you, no offense. I doubt my fear of Indians will ever pass."

"I'm just funning, is all," Chito-Ochi said. "When I disappear, I know Malvo talks about me behind my back. I must admit, I do test his patience constantly, but it keeps him on his toes. It wouldn't do getting reckless in this part of the country. This used to be a nice, quiet place, but since the Comanche went on the warpath, there's been no peace for the settlers nor anybody else that tries to pass unnoticed."

The fire sawed in the stiff breeze as sparks disappeared a few feet above the flames. Shadows danced on the trees surrounding us. I pushed a wisp of blond hair out of my blue eyes and rubbed my freckled face. It had been a long day, and I was tired.

"Always remember that the first days are a test," Chito-Ochi whispered when Malvo walked out of the night. He was not like the Choctaw, who moved silently, though. He made as much noise as a horse.

Late into the night, I awoke and eyed the strange Indian over the dying flames. He sat cross-legged with a gash for a mouth as he closed his eyes, listening to the howling wind. I wondered if he was ever going to go to sleep. The fear I felt when he was around had somehow vanished, and I wondered which one I felt safer with. It was clear they both had honorable intentions. Maybe my luck wasn't so bad after all. At least I was still breathing, and I had my hair.

The following morning, thunderclaps and a frigid breeze set the trees and bushes gnashing as we rode out and into the wind. Distant thunder quivered, and lightning slashed across the sky. Ground-shaking rumbles followed the brief streaks of electricity. Raindrops began to hammer my hat as puddles formed before my very eyes. I pulled off my cover and turned my face to the sky. Waterbombs landed on my dusty cheeks, making white streaks as they ran down.

At first, having a refreshing shower felt great, but soon, I was chilled to the bone. West Texas was known for its sudden changes in weather. Three riders' images were reflected in the standing water as hooves splashed westward. It rained so hard that my hat brim sagged to my shoulders. Lucky for me, the front held up, so I could still see.

After a few hours, the storm disappeared as quickly as it appeared, and the sun came out with a vengeance. Steam rose off the wetland, quickly drying back into dust. I took off my hat and straightened the brim as soon as it started to dry. Sunflowers' dead faces dished toward the glaring orb. As I sat on my horse, they came to my knees.

"So, where are we going? Do you really plan to go to Texas?"

"Yep," Malvo replied as he wrung out his bandana, the water dripping onto his horse's neck. "We'll ride west for a spell longer, then we'll go southwest through New Mexico. If the Lord's willin', we have a rest in a trading post about eighty miles south. I figure we can do it in two or three days, depending on the weather. That spell of rain already slowed us down some."

"The Amarillo Trading Post is a dangerous place," Chito-Ochi said. "Especially if you're an Indian."

"I reckon some of those folks have seen what I have, and it's put them off Indians. I know I was until I got to know you a little. I swear I'll never trust a Comanche, though. No, sir. Never in a thousand years."

"Never say never, son," Malvo warned. "The world is funny like that. The dangedest things happen, and as Chito-Ochi says, we have no control over what's coming. All we can do is be ready."

"Do you know how to use that pistol and the rifle?" Chito-Ochi asked. "It will not be worth much if it is only for decoration."

"I can use the rifle just fine. My pa taught me how to hunt. I can shoot as good as him, but I've never fired a pistol. My father claimed that revolvers were for shooting men and not wild game. When I took it off him, it was the first time I ever touched it. I was surprised by its weight, too. I had to use two hands to hold it up."

"If you're gonna ride with us, you'll have to learn how to use it," Malvo said. "Traveling across dangerous country means we might need our guns."

We rode through a canyon the next day and stopped by a stream. I looked at the sun. It said midday.

"We're gonna stop and have a go at some target practice," Malvo said. "That pistol won't do ya no good if ya don't know how to use it, Benji."

We pulled to a stop, and I kicked my leg over my horse's neck and slid to the ground. I was only as tall as the horse's back. When I hit the ground, I slipped in some mud left in the shadows and fell face first.

Chito-Ochi and Malvo couldn't help laughing. I pulled myself to my feet, moved out of the slush, and pushed a furrow of wet sand with the toe of my boot as I stared at the ground, embarrassed.

"Come on, young fella," Malvo said. "Wash off in the creek, and let's see what you can do with that Winchester. Let me see." He looked around for a target. "How about that dead limb over there, about a hundred yards out."

"You can make it harder than that, Malvo." I confidently smiled. "Pick out something a thousand yards away."

Chito-Ochi clucked his tongue as Malvo said, "There's a live oak beyond that cypress tree. Take a shot at the lower limb with few leaves." He shook his head in disbelief.

"If you can hit that, I'll teach you how to use that

hog iron myself"—Malvo grinned—"and I'll pay for the bullets, too."

I wiped my hands on my britches and pulled the rifle from under my saddle fender. When I put the stock to my shoulder, I thought I could smell my father. Then again, maybe my mind was playing tricks on me. I levered a round into the chamber and peered down at the sight. I carefully pulled the trigger, and the gun bucked in my hand as a bullet spat out the barrel at lightning speed. The branch in the distance exploded as wood shrapnel sprayed leaves and limbs.

"Well, I'll be a monkey's uncle," Malvo said, his mouth hanging open. "I reckon you *can* shoot, but can you handle the pistol?"

"I reckon if you teach me, I could. Like I said, I learned to outshoot my pa, and he was good with his rifle. I don't see why I can't learn to use his revolver just as well."

Malvo and Chito-Ochi smiled knowingly. "Pull that iron and let me have a look at it," Malvo said. "No offense to your father, but I want to check it out first."

When the Colt Walker single-action revolver was in Malvo's hands, it seemed like he had used it all his life. He broke it down into pieces, inspecting every feature.

"It wouldn't do to have one of these forty-four caliber slugs blow up in your face," Chito-Ochi said. "The 1847 Colt Walker has been known to do that, but don't worry, Malvo knows his weapons. He can draw fast, too. If you do as he says, you will get the feel for it in no time."

When he returned my revolver, it seemed heavier than before.

"You wanna keep an eye on the loading rammer beneath the barrel," Malvo said. "It's held in place with a spring, and if it gets worn, it'll fall with every shot and jam the cylinder from rotating. Keep that in mind, and it's still a good gun. See that little split in the hammer? It's really a notch in the hammer spur. It makes a darned good rear sight. It's got a six-shot cylinder, and each bullet holds sixty grains of black powder and a hundred-forty-eight-grain round lead ball. It has the highest muzzle velocity of any handgun made. If ya know how to use it, it's like a little cannon."

I slapped away the flies with my hat and slipped it back on. I hefted the six-shooter in my hands. I tried to hold it steady with one hand, but it wavered, so I used both hands. I thumbed back the hammer, took aim, and pulled the trigger. The blast bucked so hard that I nearly dropped the revolver. The loud bang rang loud in my ears. A rock exploded twenty-five feet away.

"Oh, my god. I never imagined it was so powerful."

"You're gonna have to exercise that right hand so you can shoot with one hand and hold your reins in the other," Malvo said. "Once we work on strengthening that arm, we can move on to the draw. When you want your gun in your hand, it's best to be fast. A split second could be the difference between life and death."

After the shooting practice, we headed for what Chito-Ochi said was a trading post. It was hard to imagine a store in such a rugged country. We rode south for eighty miles in only two days. In the distance, the land looked uninhabited, but Chito-Ochi said people were living out there somewhere, and some of them were even White.

The first night, we made camp long after nightfall. Malvo Tanner sat with his boots crossed before the fire. Chito-Ochi squatted on the ground, dangling his hands in front of him. He looked at me and smiled. I shrugged my shoulders against the West Texas evening cold.

"Tomorrow, we'll stop along the way, somewhere nobody can see us, and have another go at that pistol," Malvo said.

A slight breeze came from the north the following morning as doves called out from a thicket of greasewood.

Malvo raised his horse's hooves, undid the hobble, and slid it clear. "It's time to go, Benji."

"Where's Chito-Ochi?"

"He's gone and disappeared again, probably checking out the trail out in front of us to make sure we don't ride into trouble. Don't worry; he'll be there if we need him—he always is. It's a good thing when you have a friend you can count on and trust with your life."

"It must be."

I suddenly felt all alone again. I was even a little jealous of Malvo and Chito-Ochi's apparent friendship. Strangely enough, they seemed almost like brothers, despite one being a sunburned White man and the other a brown man with long plaits down each side of his head. Strapped across his back, he had a bow and quiver.

As we rode, I held the reins in my left hand while using a rock to strengthen my biceps, forearm, and wrist muscles. I was determined to master my father's pistol just like I did his Winchester rifle. I exercised my arm until it went numb.

five
the trading post

"We are only a few hours away from the Amarillo Trading Post," Chito-Ochi said. "If the Comanche don't kill everybody or run them out, it might become a small town someday."

When he crept up behind us, I nearly jumped out of my saddle. Even his horse was uncannily quiet, and I felt my mount shiver his coat.

"Who knows," Malvo replied. "As mean as the folks are around there, they might kill each other before the Comanche get to them."

"I swear, Chito-Ochi, you could sneak up on a ghost."

To our right, the sun began its descent at the end of the world. When it touched the horizon, it exploded into a prism of colors. In minutes, darkness fell around us, but we continued to follow Chito-Ochi, who uncannily seemed to be able to see in the dark. The only light was from stars light years away. The clopping of hooves sounded lonely in the night.

The horses cantered nervously as we roweled them on blindly.

When we finally rode into the trading post compound, it smelled of freshly sawn lumber—a half dozen shoats roasted on spits mixing odors. The cooking figures shined black in the firelight, and the coals glowed underneath. The smell of cooked food floated on puffs of air, making my mouth water. A dog fight broke out over charred hog bones. I heard a gunshot, and one of the canines howled in pain, running for cover.

We wheeled our horses following the pale band of light on the floorboard of the tavern and store coming from the door. A rumble of noise emitted from inside the large log building. Squares of light spilled out of two pane glass windows, shining yellow squares on the ground.

Ladies of the Night hung out on a small balcony on the second story. Their faces were painted with indigo and pale powder, looking gaudy. Patchouli oil lingered heavily in the air, overpowering all other smells. They hid their faces behind hand fans, as their eyes blinked with lurid coyness.

Many in the trading post bar wore long mustaches and wide-brimmed hats with high crowns. The man behind the bar was as bald as a stone and had long, bushy sideburns that started from nothing at his ears, matching his thick nose hair and eyebrows.

The two Indians who sat in the back looked like mud effigies as they eyed us when we entered. A pot of coffee sat on their table with two tin cups and a sugar bowl. Without looking, one mixed scoop after scoop into the steaming, black liquid.

"Let's go have a whiskey." Malvo grinned as he walked ten paces to the bar. "Did your pa ever invite ya to a drink of liquor?"

"No, sir, he didn't believe in drinking. The only reason we didn't go to church was that there weren't any, but Pa read from the Bible nightly."

"Well, let me be the first to invite you to a shot. It'll be my honor. Barkeep, set us up with three glasses and a bottle. We'll pay as we go."

The man behind the bar marked the bottle with a piece of white chalk. He placed that and three glasses on the bar top and waited to be paid. Malvo tossed a nickel and a dime, clattering on the hewn wood.

Mr. Tanner turned to me and held out his fist, dropping ten coins into my hand. I stared at them in my palm without moving a muscle, finally cupping the dimes like a bird. I looked up at Malvo and smiled. I could feel my eyes twinkle.

"A man can't walk around with empty pockets." Malvo chuckled. "From the look on your face, you've never had any money, either. We'll call that a loan."

He poured a shot glass full for each of us, including Chito-Ochi. When he did, the bartender frowned, but one look from Malvo shut his mouth tight. I'd never seen that look in his eyes before. It sent a shiver up my spine. Now I understood what the Choctaw Indian was on about Tanner's mother being a scorpion. Yet, I felt no aggression toward me at all.

"Salud, as they say in Mexico." Malvo grinned as we touched glasses.

Both men tossed theirs back in one go. I looked them in the eyes and felt I had to do the same. I sniffed the alcohol, and it wrinkled my nose, but despite the bad smell, I knew I had to drink it. I was supposed to be a man now.

I drained my glass and nearly choked. I had to excuse myself and go outside to keep from being embarrassed. Boot heels quickly pounded the saloon wood plank floor. I stepped to the edge of the porch and tried to spit out the taste. It burned as much coming back up as it did going down. I blinked the tears from my eyes as I swallowed again. After taking a few deep breaths, I turned for the door. As I walked to the bar, a warm tingling hit my stomach. It was pleasant. Then, that same warmth snaked through my mind, making me grin.

"It's powerful, but after I got over the bad taste, it feels just fine."

Both of my new friends busted out laughing until they were holding their sides. Malvo gave me a wicked grin and poured the shot glasses full again.

"One more before we get something to eat." Chito-Ochi snickered. "I never have more than two shots because it affects my good judgment."

Surprisingly, the second shot went down much easier, and I didn't have to spit any out. That warm, tingling feeling coursed through my body, making me glow. Suddenly, I was famished.

"What did you say about supper?"

"That boy could eat a man out of house and home." Malvo laughed.

I finally felt divested of all I had felt and seen. Suddenly, my origins seemed to become as remote as my destiny. We made our way to a table in what they would call the diner. We took empty seats in the back near the dark Indians as they continued to stare. Strangely enough, Malvo and even Chito-Ochi ignored them as though they weren't even there.

Malvo finally motioned toward the Indians in the corner with a swing of his eyes and raised eyebrows while I sat as mute as a mannequin. When the Indian waiter came, Chito-Ochi held up three fingers. He brought three plates of ribs and three bowls of pork stew in minutes. I sniffed my plate as steam blurred my eyes, and my stomach grumbled. Three mugs of warm beer accompanied it.

"You sit tight, and we'll be back in a minute," Malvo said, surprising me. It sounded more like an order.

"But what about your food?"

But it was too late. They disappeared out the door. The only ones watching appeared to be the two Indians sitting at a nearby table. I could feel their stares as they drilled into my mind.

"You're no better than them, are ya? What White man runs with an Indian? Why, you're no more than a boy."

"What? Are you talking to me?"

I wrapped my hand around the butt of my holstered pistol. A sudden anxiousness overcame me, and my heart beat nervously between my ears. My eyes grew as soon as I saw one of the Indians stand. He motioned me away from the table with his chin. My control of the moment was wrenched from my grasp, making my insides knot together as alarm bells rang in my brain. My heart suddenly began to thump in my throat. I had no idea what to do next.

The Indian barely shrugged, evincing a hint of a smile as he lay a pistol on the table and moved away, pulling a knife.

I tried to reach into my boot for my knife as we were suddenly circling crabwise. Sweat streamed down my face. I couldn't believe what I'd gotten myself into, and I was only left alone for minutes. Should I pull my gun and shoot even though it was clearly a knife fight? And why did this Indian want to kill me? Or was it just a ruse? Puzzlement filled my brain as my breath came short and fast.

I squeezed my fists, feeling the blood come to a stop in my veins, and my fingernails dug into my palms. Right then, my stomach fell off a cliff. My eyes stretched wide as I locked eyes with the Cheyenne Indian.

"Oh, my god."

I instantly saw Tanner and the Choctaw in my peripheral vision. The cage of Malvo's eyes was like red wires. The blow from his fist doubled the Indian over. A moan came from deep inside as his breath whooshed out, and he sank to his knees.

I gasped when Malvo pulled his pistol and aimed it at the Cheyenne Indian. The click of the hammer was loud in the closed room. It came out of his holster so quickly it was a blur. He swung the barrel, telling him to leave, and nodded at his friend.

"You two best clear on out of here right now before I change my mind and shoot ya both for good measure," Malvo said in just over a whisper. "And make sure you don't come back until we leave. Do you understand?" He drummed his fingers on his pistol grips like he had an itch and wanted to scratch it. "Next time you see my young friend here, just make out like he's me, and you won't get killed."

Chito-Ochi repeated everything in broken Cheyenne, and they solemnly nodded. They got up and scampered away. Neither one looked my way.

"Is that stew any good?" Chito-Ochi asked as if nothing happened. He completely ignored the incident.

"I could eat a bear," Malvo Tanner said, but now his voice was edgier.

I wondered what they were up to. Lucky for me, they weren't gone long, or they might have found me bleeding out on the tavern floor. I drew in a deep breath, sniffled, and shook my head. That instant rage I felt dropped away, and my pulse calmed like a receding tide. I warily looked at my two new friends and wondered how long it would last.

I spooned some stew into my mouth, and the flavor exploded, making me smile. For me, the only thing that overrode every instinct was my stomach. Of course, I was still a growing teenager.

"I reckon it's pretty good." I pulled a rib off the

rack and popped it into my mouth, drawing the bone out with my fingers. "The ribs are mighty tasty, too."

The only sound for the next few minutes was spoons scraping against wooden bowls. Chito-Ochi kept his on a pigging string hanging around his neck. It looked like everybody had their own spoon but me.

"Now that I have a little money, where can I buy a spoon?" I raised my eyebrows. "This wooden one is rough on my mouth."

"With the way you eat, it does not surprise me," Chito-Ochi said, smiling, while chewing a mouthful.

"You can buy one for a nickel in the trading post tomorrow," Malvo said. "Always keep it on you. It's almost as important as your gun. To have the energy to protect yourself, you've got to eat."

I wiped my bowl and tin pie pan clean with a chunk of white bread and popped it in my mouth. I, too, spoke with a full mouth.

"So, what riled those two Indians up so much? They seemed to know you both."

"A lot more people know us than we know them," Malvo said. "That, my boy, is called a reputation. Sometimes, it's a good thing to have; sometimes, it's not so good. Be forewarned; if you ride with us, one day you might have one, too."

Again, I asked myself, who was this man? He was seemingly kind and generous to me, but at the same time, I felt something dangerous behind those green eyes. He mentioned he hadn't cut his beard since the end of the war. What did the conflict mean for him, and did he still have political feelings? Or was all that killed in the many battles they had survived? Subtle scars were there to see if a person looked close enough. I'd seen them myself in my father when he let his guard down.

Why did they seem so familiar to me, and why didn't they leave me back at the burned ranch? There were so many questions and so few answers. I still didn't feel free to pry into their private lives. My life had been laid bare for everyone to see. At this point, these two strangers knew me better than anyone else in the world. I wondered how all this would pan out in the next days, weeks, and months. Would I last that long?

Now that I was on the trail, I realized how much of a greenhorn I was. It was a mysterious miracle that I was still alive, and now I found myself at the mercy of two men I don't even know.

The way the people in the saloon looked at them rang alarm bells in my brain. It was like they knew who Malvo and Chito-Ochi were even though they hadn't met. At this point, I didn't know what to do except go with the flow. Now, they were my only friends, but maybe we weren't good friends, I thought. Only time would tell.

All this confusion made me seem even younger than I was—somehow more vulnerable. I'm fourteen and going on twenty-five. I had the feeling that my childhood was long lost, but now I had to wait to see what I become as a man. I wondered if my new friends would be a part of my education or if they would be the end of my life as I knew it.

Malvo *was* right about one thing. There was no way to ever turn back the clock. There was only one way to go now: forward, any way I could. Would I stay with the two men with a reputation, or would I strike out on my own? I still didn't have the answer to that. I didn't even know if I would any time soon. I had lost control of things days ago. I wondered if I would ever have my old life back again.

war parties

Five Comanche warriors sat patiently under a silvery moon. A small fire crackled and popped. Each one had a willow stick with a piece of meat on the end, roasting over orange coals. The odor of roasted meat was strong in the air. Smoke squirreled into the sky, disappearing instantly in the dark. Moon shadows stood long beside the sitting men as they patiently stared into the distance.

Shiny black scalps hung from their belts. Some were still fresh and bloody. Blowflies hovered overhead. The leader had their only gun. It was a Spencer rifle but was nothing when compared to Winchester. They also carried arrows and lances. The Comanche could fire an arrow every two to three seconds. Only a double-action revolver or a Winchester rifle could handle such rapid fire.

The warriors wore loincloths and painted faces. Their hair hung below their shoulders, and their skin was burned a dark red from the fierce Texan sun. Each appeared more frightening than the other. No one spoke a word as they waited. The only sound was the nightly choir of coyotes and the crackling fire.

They saw the packs' silhouettes on the distant ridges against a pumpkin moon, which reflected in the Comanches' dead-pan eyes. Long lances protruded from the ground within their reach, and war clubs lay beside them. There was no question of what they were up to. They had come prepared for war.

The war chief slipped bullets into the loading magazine, fumbling with the brass casings. Another sat grinding his razor-sharp knife against a whetstone. It produced the slightest sound, only auditable from feet away, like the bullets clicking as they were loaded into the rifle.

The hooves of five horses clopped into the small, dark campsite—the tiny fire cast shadows on the surrounding trees. The leader of the second war party nodded and sat beside the others, as mute as stones. Two hours later, the first light of a new day began to emerge and shoo away the shadows. The third war party came into the camp in broad daylight, and all fifteen men jumped into action.

They unhobbled and mounted their ponies, and formed a long line as they snaked over dry, dusty trails toward the White men's trading post. The place had been mentioned in Indian rumors for some time. If these Comanche warriors had their way, they would run them off or kill them before the moon rose that night.

Their intelligence of the situation was close to

nothing, but they still felt confident. Everybody was afraid of the warrior tribe, so they didn't expect these White people to be any different. How many could live in such tight quarters? Their intel on the size of the building was wrong, but they would soon find out.

Despite Indians from various tribes constantly visiting the trading post, the fifteen-strong war party had spoken to no one who had been inside or even nearby. All they knew was that White men had set up a place to trade goods with the Indians and other trespassers like the one who ran the business. All they had heard about the proprietor was that he had a hairy face and bald head and lots of White men's money.

Some said the trading post was teeming with pistols and rifles for sale and had a good stock of lead balls and black powder. These rumors made it to the north of the Red River. The war party's leader wondered how he would take the bald man's scalp. Perhaps he could remove the hair from his face. There was no light save the fire.

As the sun blazed overhead, the Comanche disregarded the heat. To them, it was just another day. They ignored all discomfort and focused one hundred percent on their target. If they were lucky, they dreamed of stealing a significant cache of firearms to take back to their chief. They could arm every man in the war party with fifteen rifles or pistols. Most of them didn't know how to use them but were after the prestige that owning one brought. It was time to fight fire with fire. This would leave them on an even playing field.

With the repeating rifles, they could run the White men entirely off the Plains and kill any who resisted and refused to leave. When they came to where the White man's camp was supposed to be, the three war chiefs sneaked out to see what they were up against while the others hid in the brush, waiting for their signal. If they couldn't hit them during the day, they would always have another chance just after dark.

When they got close enough to see the trading post, they were surprised by the number of people. A mixture of white, black, and red men was seen preparing to leave or just arriving. They knew Indians traded there, but they didn't expect there to be so many. The warriors exchanged looks and backed away into the dense foliage. When they were far enough away, they jumped to their feet and ran.

sound the alarm

That night, we slept in a rickety bunkhouse built onto the back of the trading post. I looked more like an afterthought than a plan. Still, most of the bunks were filled with smelly, sunburnt men. Everybody had a pistol under their straw mattress or pillow, and I was no exception.

Leather saddles swung gently from ropes through the rafters, and harnesses hung on bunk bed posts. Cowboys with big Stubben spurs filled the many beds. I heard mice scurry across the wood plank floor. They didn't seem to be afraid of humans. Here in the trading post, they must have plenty to eat. I wrinkled my nose as an old man nearby passed the wind. For a second, I remembered back home, where I had a fine straw mattress and a comfortable place to sleep. I hadn't slept a peaceful night for days.

My rifle lay along my side, hidden under my blanket, with a round levered into the chamber. My Colt Walker was under a rolled-up blanket I used as a pillow.

The lump of metal against my ear made me feel safer. Lucky for me, I was sleeping in the bunk over Malvo.

Chito-Ochi had disappeared again hours before, but Tanner didn't mention it, and the Indian never said when or where he was going. It was a mystery to me. I wonder if he didn't like to sleep with so many White strangers, or was he off on one of his scouting excursions? I had no idea, since he rarely commented on where he had gone or what he did.

Crowing roosters awoke me the following day. I was surprised to see sunlight spilling into the bunkhouse window. It looked like I'd slept into the morning. I swung my head over the edge of my bunk and looked for Malvo, but he wasn't there. I blinked when I realized I was alone. There was no sign of anybody. The few agonizing moments it took me to gather my things and head for the door seemed to stretch into minutes rather than seconds. Eventually, it seemed like an hour before I burst into the sunlight.

When my boot heels hammered the porch, I heard people whispering about Comanche. The blood drained from my face. I wasn't ready for a second encounter with the most feared Indian on the Plains.

I propped my rifle against the wall and hurriedly strapped on my revolver. Malvo and Chito-Ochi were already on the porch, sitting at a wooden table, putting fresh rounds into their weapons. They had somber looks on their faces, which accompanied thousand-yard stares. A bottle of whiskey and three glasses sat beside the bullets. Two were empty, and one was full. The

Choctaw filled the bullet belts he strapped across his chest.

"You better get ready, Benji," Malvo warned. There was a sudden seriousness about the way he talked. "We might need the extra firepower, especially as you're a crack shot. I saved ya a little whiskey. Today, it'll serve as medicine and calm your nerves. Just enough to take the edge off things but not so much as to affect our aim. This is an exception and not a rule of thumb. We only drink on special occasions, and most men facing battle can use a little nip of liquor to strengthen their determination."

"Maybe they won't come once they see how big the trading post is." I crossed my fingers against all odds.

"*Maybe* ain't a word that applies to the Comanche," Malvo said. "If they're coming, they'll be coming hard, and there's no way they'll turn back. That ain't their way."

"There is a sizable war party of fifteen Comanche braves riding toward the trading post right here," Chito-Ochi said. "I followed them all night."

I blinked my eyes in disbelief. It took a madman to follow Comanche Indians willingly. I looked around and noticed everyone was scrambling for cover, and they were all armed with pistols *and* rifles. Some men dove under the trading post porch. I could see the barrels of their guns tremble below my boots. Only Malvo and Chito-Ochi refused to hide. Compared to my facial expression, they didn't appear scared at all as they stared in the distance with hard eyes.

A shudder raced through my body, making my

teeth chatter. Malvo gave me a questioning look and seemed to chuckle before he turned his attention back to the trail.

I suddenly felt utterly vulnerable. Was I sitting next to two madmen? Yet, Chito-Ochi apparently warned the trading post owners and clients of the imminent danger. That alone would save lives. Were these men dangerous killers, or did they uphold moral laws and good people? Sometimes, I believed they were honest men, but then they mentioned something that sounded violent, and I questioned myself again. I knew Malvo didn't hesitate to shoot if threatened. His guns weren't for show.

Maybe there's more to Chito-Ochi and Malvo than there appears. I wonder if I'll ever figure them out.

"If they don't swing around and try to flank us, they should come from right over there," Malvo said, pointing a long finger. He almost sounded bored. "Turn those other tables on their sides. The wood should be thick enough to stop most projectiles except for lances. Their spears will cut through the wooden tops like butter. It'll give us a place to hide if they shoot a cloud of arrows, though. It's anybody's guess if they have guns or not."

"I only saw three," Chito-Ochi said. "One each for the war chiefs. A rifle and two revolvers, but that does not mean they work or have many bullets. Guns are hard to come by in the Indian Territories and are often broken. I rarely see an Indian who knows how to shoot anyway. None of them have money to spend on black powder to practice. I would focus on the men with arrows and lances. That will be the main threat."

I admit, I wasn't as brave as my new friends, so I ducked behind one of the tables I turned on their sides. I clamped my teeth together to keep them from chattering more. I levered a round into the chamber, poked the barrel over the top, and had a look. I could already see where riding men kicked up a cloud of dust. The blurry images of brightly painted faces reminded me of not too long ago.

"This one's for you, James," I whispered.

I had a one-in-a-million shot, especially since they were moving at a gallop. I licked my finger and held it up, checking the direction of the wind. I sniffled and drew a breath. My heartbeat was full of dread. I peeked over, and bright sunlight flashed in my eyes. My blood sped into overdrive as I squinted down the long barrel and to the gun sight. Suddenly, I felt something strange. Maybe it was revenge.

I let out a long, slow breath as I focused on the painted man leading the war party. He appeared to be riding through a park, not toward twenty armed men. I gently applied pressure to the trigger, and the gun bucked hard against my shoulder, nearly making me drop it, but even though I was small, I was strong.

I saw a powder flash beside me, and gun smoke followed a lead slug out of the barrel. I waited—it seemed like a minute. The Comanche toppled backward off his horse. Blood sprayed the brave behind him as he, too, fell. The bullet passed through the first rider and into the second. Two of our enemies were down with a single shot. The first one was dead before he hit the ground. Malvo's bullet struck home but mine missed. I was shaking too hard to aim straight.

I was waiting to see if I felt anything like jubilation or success. I had, after all, just attempted to take revenge for my brother, James, but the only thing that hit my stomach was dread. Still, I knew it was their lives or ours. I hadn't meant to start the battle, though. It was my gunshot and miss that had set it off.

Malvo Tanner looked at me, surprised, scratching his bushy beard, and squinting intelligent eyes. "Attaway! You almost got 'em!" he yelled, slapping his knee. "Didn't I tell you this boy had what it takes? Go on, keep on shootin'. There ain't nothin' shy about hostile Indians."

Chito-Ochi was painted from head to toe in dark red and green with slashes of yellow. He looked like a clay voodoo doll. I blinked in wonder as I tried to keep my hands from trembling while levering another round into the chamber. I didn't know who scared me more, the Comanche or the Choctaw.

In the distance, the Comanche seemed to have delved into confusion as they wheeled their horses chaotically. Finally, the second war chief took the leader's place, and the ponies ran recklessly. They raced directly for us. When all the men's guns went off, it sounded like popcorn in a skillet. Warriors got knocked over like carnival dolls. Twenty guns roared like some crazed beast.

The surviving warriors wheeled their horses back from where they came and raced away with half the original numbers. Dead bodies littered the ground two hundred yards in front of the trading post. The acrid smell of blood filled the air, while I gritted my teeth to keep them still.

"That should send them back to where they came," Malvo huffed, slipping off his hat and wiping his brow with his sleeve.

"For your first time that was not bad, Benji," Chito-Ochi said. "You only have to learn to stay calm and it will get easier, and you will shoot straighter."

"It was some bully shot, Malvo, and you got two of them with a single bullet." I grinned at him like he was my father.

For a moment, I wondered if that was what this was all about. Malvo Tanner didn't have any family—or at least he never talked about having a wife or children. I reckon Chito-Ochi was sort of like his kin. Maybe he never had a family like regular folks. I've noticed that, at times, he called me son and looked at me with what I believed were almost loving eyes. Then again, they were still strangers, and maybe I was just seeing what I wanted to see.

I also remembered what I saw in his eyes when he challenged the Cheyenne Indian bothering me at the bar. I've never seen a father with a look like that. It sent cold chills up my spine.

Men with rifles crawled from under the porch, dusting off their clothing with their hats. Three men carefully rode out to check on the Indians. Maybe they were making sure they weren't alive. I'm sort of glad some of them got away, and I don't even know why.

The riders returned, yelling at the top of their lungs and waving their hats in the air in victory. I didn't particularly feel victorious. My pulse raced a million miles a minute, and that bad feeling in my stomach spread.

Maybe I wasn't cut out to ride with men like Malvo and Chito-Ochi. I've never met anyone like them, so I'm having difficulty figuring things out.

Malvo snapped his fingers before my eyes and said, "Come on, snap out of it. I know it's hard because it's your first battle, but as you well know, we had no choice. Those men were coming to kill us, and what put some sand into the gears was our gunfire. Considering the circumstances, you did as well as any young greenhorn I've ever seen."

I didn't quite know if I liked being called a greenhorn but the compliment felt fine just the same.

eight
the aftermath

Once the Comanche war party retreated, disappearing in a cloud of dust, the men in the shadows and under the building came out blinking in wonder. They looked surprised to be alive—just like me. I felt like pinching myself to make sure but was embarrassed somebody would notice.

Today was another first for me. I'd never shot a man before. Hopefully, there will never be a second time. It happened so fast I didn't feel about it as I had suspected. It was as easy as pulling the trigger. Of course, the enemy was at a distance, so it wasn't up close and personal. Still, I didn't feel the dread and grief I expected. When the time came, I went mechanical, like an engine. All the parts worked on their own with no thought.

Was that how Malvo and Chito-Ochi felt when they had to act? Or did they do it because they liked killing as though it were a habit? The answer to that remained to be seen. I knew I didn't like it, though, and

I never wanted to do it again. My pa's rifle felt like a ton of bricks, and the heavy revolver pulled at my waist. What kind of world had I stepped into? I wasn't prepared for what was to come unless I learned fast. This may not be the last time my life got threatened.

I was torn between wanting to hide like a boy or buck up to the consequences and once and for all become a man. I knew I wasn't a child any longer, so I only really had one choice. I was fourteen years old, going on twenty-five. I was going to have to grow up quickly. If that meant following Malvo and Chito-Ochi's directions to the letter, until I learned enough to head out on my own, that was what I was going to do.

From then on, I began to study their actions to the finest detail—right or wrong. That and I started to ask questions about everything I didn't understand or wanted to know more about. The Choctaw Indian proved to be a treasure trove of information. He knew everything about birds, mammals, and reptiles. He even told me some of them talk, although I had never seen it happen. Maybe he was kidding me, but with Indians, you just never knew.

Malvo continued to work on my shooting skills with my .44-caliber Colt. I had exercised my right arm enough to hold it in one hand while firing. I was even getting a little faster with my draw. I was surprised at the damage this weapon packed. It wasn't the most powerful handgun in the world for nothing. Even Tanner said it was a small cannon. Once I got used to using it, I would have an edge. I figured, at worst, I could shoot bullets through doors.

That night, everybody in the dining room was talking about one hostile Indian attack or another. I was surprised so many people had stories. Of course, none of them were as explicit as mine, or they wouldn't have been there to tell it. I just got away by the skin on my chin. Smoke hovered overhead a foot below the ceiling. Shiny spittoons scattered across the floor, but the customers were obviously poor shots. Brown stains covered the floor around the bright brass.

The room was nearly complete. Only a single table remained unoccupied. We rushed over and sat down before somebody else took it. A dozen smells assaulted my senses—so many that it was hard to single one out. To the far side, two card games were in motion. Two tables had empty chairs. Malvo craned his head to see who was playing. A strange light lit up in his eyes.

"Maybe I'll have a hand at cards after dinner while you two snoop around," Malvo said, then looked at Chito-Ochi. "I promise, small stakes only, pard."

"What are we snooping for? I'm gonna need to know what I'm looking for to find something."

"Work," Malvo replied. He raised his hand and motioned to the bartender. When he got the man's attention, he raised three fingers and rolled his finger. He wanted to say the same as yesterday.

I smelled the bear stew suspiciously, but my mouth began to water when it hit my senses. Food had to be bad for me to pass, but this actually smelled delicious.

"This is the first time I've eaten bear meat. It smells just fine."

"You seem to be saying that a lot lately." Malvo smiled.

"What is that?"

"This is the first time..." His smile turned into a grin, and Chito-Ochi chuckled.

"If he tells us it's the first time every time he discovers something new, we are going to get bored." The Choctaw Indian laughed. "But don't worry, Benji. I have endless patience. If I didn't, I wouldn't ride with Malvo."

"I know I'm still green, but you just watch. I'm a fast learner. In no time, I'll be keeping up."

nine
heading south

I removed my bedroll and rifle, uncinched and threw down my saddle, hobbling my horse foreleg to rear as my two new friends did likewise. We always tended to the animals before making camp, leaving the saddles and bridles nearby in case we needed them fast. These were strange habits, but I did as was told. I was the one who needed more experience. I might survive the month if I listened to what my elders said.

But when we get to El Paso, maybe I'll decide that is as far as I want to go. It must be safer there than here on the trail.

So far, it had been a precarious journey, and if I continued, I doubted the danger would end. Trouble seemed to follow Malvo and Chito-Ochi like flies followed manure. Or was it *me* that trouble was following around everywhere we went? It *was* my family's farm that got attacked. Malvo and the Choctaw came to save me, I suppose. I hope it wasn't me who was bringing them all the grief. I guess I still believed in luck, but all we'd gotten lately was bad. A little good luck would be good for a change.

As I watched overhead, the stars swung counter-clockwise in their nightly course as the Big Bear turned. The star Earendel winked in the farthest distance—the sky was that clear. A dozen falling stars left vapor trails streaking brightly toward Earth. They burned out in midair.

I lay back as I stared at the heavens, wondering what was in store for me next. At this point, I had little choice because I had no control over what happened and no place else to go. When I rode out, the remains of my home were no more than ashes.

I only rode along with Malvo and Chito-Ochi because they turned up and offered. What would I have done if they rode off and left me? My scalp would prob-ably be on some Comanche's belt.

It was my turn to take guard duty. I had the last three hours before dawn. The rising sun found me crouched under a large boulder. I sat for a spell, maybe more, before I heard Malvo and Chito-Ochi stir. A small group of wolves moved up the far side of the next arroyo, looking for something to eat.

I sat, leaning with my back against a boulder. The heat from yesterday was still glowing from the rock, and the first rays of sun warmed my face. The sky burst into a pink, rose, and crimson prism, quickly stretching to the other horizon. Heat wavered across the land as the yellow disc came into full view.

That was when I heard something rustling in the bushes. At first, it sounded like a raccoon or some small animal. The noise came again, and this time, it was closer. I clutched my pistol grip in my right hand. Now, whatever I heard didn't seem so small.

I blinked when I saw the outline of a man with a big hat and a long gun. He crept softly into our camp, remembering the long shadows made by the early morning sun. He hadn't seen me yet.

When the hammer on my revolver clicked, it was loud enough for the intruder to hear. The stranger froze for a split second, then swung his gun barrel my way. I got caught out with no time to act.

My mouth went as dry as a desert as my hand began to raise my pistol, but I knew I was too late. He got the drop on me, and I was supposed to be the guard. I had failed my friends, and above all, I failed myself, and it would now cost me my life.

Everything that had happened in the last few days flashed before my eyes. I felt the muscle in my right arm respond as it pulled on the heavy iron, but it felt like I was moving in slow motion. I tried to will the gun out but to no avail.

Malvo suddenly came up and out of his blanket. He had his pistols in his fists. One gun discharged into the chest of the man who snuck into our camp. The loud bang brought me to my senses, and I realized how hard I was squeezing my grip. I had just cleared leather.

The gunshot man had pink froth on his lips. I saw a neat hole in his chest. The one on his back was gaping and jagged. He lay on his side, trying to gobble air, but found none. His mouth was full of blood. The range was so close, the cloth surrounding the bullet hole smoked and began to burn.

My heart was sprinting, and my mind was jumbled and confused, but I knew I had to keep my head. Right now, it was all about survival. My anger flared, and again, my mind spun despite my struggle for control. I craned my neck to look behind me and saw Malvo with a brace of six guns in his fists.

A stream of smoke squirreled out of one gun barrel. The look in his eyes sent a shudder through me like a small earthquake. I could swear I saw tombstones in his eyes. I blinked repeatedly, and they disappeared.

That can't be. I must have been seeing things.

Lately, I don't quite know what to think.

"You're gonna have to kick it up a notch or two, Benji," Malvo warned. "Hadn't I been here, you might have ended up dead. When you hesitate, even for an instant, you put your life at peril and ours with it. It would help if you had shot this rascal as soon as you saw him step into camp with a gun. An honest man will call out first and not brandish irons. Next time, don't wait for me, just shoot. That's why we have a night guard, son."

Embarrassed, I could feel the red climb from my neck to my cheeks. I hadn't held up my end of the deal and nearly got myself killed. Malvo was right; I would have to kick it up a notch or two if I wanted to survive.

"I'm sorry about that, sir. I won't let it happen again. Who was it anyway?" I looked at him determinedly.

"There are often thieves along the trail to El Paso,

and I reckon he was one of them," Malvo said as he rifled the man's pockets and took his guns. "Maybe if we snoop around a spell, we might find his horse. There's no sense letting horseflesh go to waste if it's any good."

"Most thieves have fast horses to run away from the place of their crime, and I am short of one animal," Chito-Ochi said. "One more mount won't do us any harm unless we run short on water, but I'm pretty good at finding springs and creeks."

"Did you know they call El Paso the six-gun capital of the world?" Malvo snickered. "The Mexican side is even more dangerous. It's a town called Juarez."

"Great. That's all I needed. I hoped there would be some law and order where we're going. I guess that chicken already flew the coop."

"Chicken—coop?" Chito-Ochi asked. "I don't understand."

"It doesn't matter. I just thought El Paso sounded like a friendly place is all. I reckon I was wrong again. In that case, I ain't in no hurry to arrive. We can take all the time you want. I have no cravings for more violence."

Malvo dragged the dead body into the bushes and then counted the money the thief had in his wallet.

"This must be one of them prosperous outlaws," Malvo said. "He had nearly a hundred dollars on him. It's not a fortune but pays for the bother and the bullet. I guess it will have to do."

I watched as Tanner shoved the money into his britches pocket. If my guess was right, he didn't give the thief's death another thought. It was as though it never happened. Chito-Ochi was the same. He hardly even looked up when Malvo shot the man point blank.

It nearly shocked me to death. I thought my heart would jump out of my chest when it happened. I wondered if the fear still showed on my face. That was too close for comfort.

Where was I? Why was everything so wild and dangerous? Now, seeing what I have, I can't fathom how my family survived so long on the Red River without being killed the first month. Every time something happened, it just confirmed my survival of the Comanche attack on my family was indeed a miracle, just like Malvo said. There wasn't any other word for it.

A half-hour later, Malvo was snoring softly like he'd never been awoken and shot a man dead. Chito-Ochi had disappeared again, but now I was getting used to it. Somehow, I felt safer when he was out there in the dark. I lay staring at the stars like tiny dots of fire, sparkling from incalculable distances.

I don't know when I fell asleep. I woke up to the smell of Chito-Ochi's frying pan biscuits. My mouth began to water before I remembered what happened. Then my tongue suddenly felt thick and turned as dry as dirt.

Later that day, the sun shone on the high hills where we stood, and the wind came off the desert. The sand lay in deep pockets on the sloping country before us. We floundered down slopes the best we could, leading the horses on foot.

Gnarled   mesquite   trees   and   naked   rocks

surrounded by rubble and stone ran down the other side. I struggled for a purchase and nearly slid to the bottom before I grabbed a root and pulled myself to a stop. My horses slid behind me. In a panic, I felt my pistol holster, but my gun was still there.

For the horses, there were sparse tufts of grass among the wildly scattered cactus plants and mesquite trees. When we reached the top of the mountain, we lay on our stomachs, crawling to the edge and skylighting the terrain for danger. We lay there for an hour but saw nothing moving, yet I felt we were being watched. Or was it my old friend, paranoia, sitting on my shoulder again?

Trees stood like ghosts on the desert floor, and pencil-line shadows stood long beside them, making them appear larger than they were.

Small ground owls crouched wing to wing as beaded lizards with black mouths scurried across rocks. The venomous reptiles stared at us with one eye before scrambling for safety, not knowing it was more dangerous than humans.

"Stuff your pants legs into your boots, Benji," Malvo said as he studied the land before us. "It'll keep rattlers from crawling up your britches and biting you. Your high leather boots will protect your ankles."

"But I'm wearing chaps. They should be enough."

"Do as you're told until you are old enough to get by on your own." Chito-Ochi smiled. I could tell he liked me and didn't want to offend. "The back of your chaps is open, and you don't want a rattler to strike your calves. They will bite you several times if you step into a nest."

I swung into the worn saddle and clucked my horse forward. We spent days riding where no souls ventured, save us. The wind ransacked the trees around us as the nestling birds cried out, clutching limbs for dear life.

Occasionally, I would see one of the spare horses stop and sway in the stiff wind. They usually followed us without a lead now, but sometimes, one got lazy, and we had to go back and fetch it. We rode from breakfast to supper with only the occasional rest for the horses. Malvo and Chito-Ochi never seemed to tire.

I was the first one up for a change. When I checked on the animals, I found one of my two horses on the ground, struggling to get up. I cinched a belt around its muzzle and slipped onto its back as it rose. It stood with its legs spread, trembling.

I slipped the belt off his mouth, grabbed a fist full of mane, and rode on its raw spine around the camp until it got its confidence back. I could feel its vertebrae as they moved under the hide. I might be young, but I know my horses. Slipping off, I pulled up my chaps and tightened my belt. It was the weight of my pistol that pulled at my britches. The horse's teeth glowed in the firelight. In an hour, we were back on the never-ending trail.

Later that day, my weakening horse slipped off the ledge at the edge of the trail, and it slammed to the ground so hard blood shot out of its ears. When it hit, it broke its forelegs. The ten-foot fall was more than it could take. I tied my horse and skinned down the gravelly slope to the bottom. The horse's lungs sounded like a broken steam engine. I pulled my Colt, drew back the hammer, and fired a shot into its brain to put it out of its misery.

I immediately began skinning its hindquarters so we could cut some steaks off the rump. A few minutes later, Malvo and Chito-Ochi were beside me, each with a skinning knife in their hands. On the Texan plains, nothing went to waste.

"We can roast what we want to eat today over the fire, and the rest we can put on salt," Chito-Ochi said. "That will cover our food needs for the next few days."

As soon as we walked away, a pair of vultures began to trot toward the fresh meat, their wings outheld, like they were ready to take flight at the slightest danger. Their ugly heads jerked obscenely. They hardly allowed us time to finish. Another dozen circled not too far above. Two tucked their wings and dove like rockets, pulling their air brakes at the last moment as they spread their ten-foot wings.

My horse shifted its hooves nervously and backed up. The smell of blood made its nostrils flare.

ten
u.s. cavalry

Malvo and Chito-Ochi pulled out collapsible spy glasses as they studied the cloud of dust in the distance.

"What is it?"

"You mean, who is it," Chito-Ochi replied.

"Right now, your guess is as good as mine," Malvo said. "But those are horses, and I'd be surprised if somebody wasn't riding them."

Even though they seemed nearby, it took us a half day to ride close enough to check them out. Out here, distances were deceiving. The second time we pulled up, I could make out the uniforms. At least they weren't Comanche or Apache, which I'd heard about, too.

I didn't want to have anything to do with either one of the tribes. Both were known to be brutal and violent, but I doubted any of them were as terrifying as the bunch that burned my family's home.

"It's Bluecoats," Chito-Ochi said. The way he said it made me a little nervous. He fought during the war right beside Malvo, both for the South. "I count twenty men plus the officers. It looks like they might be lost." The Indian chuckled at the folly. "I wonder who they are looking for."

"I hope they aren't looking for us." Nobody seemed to hear me.

"Whatcha think they're doin' out here?" Malvo asked.

"Looking for that bunch of Comanche would be my guess," the Choctaw replied. "Either that or that thief you killed."

"I wish they'd have showed up when those rascals hit our place. Maybe they could have saved our ranch."

"The way I see it, you were already too lucky," Malvo said. "Nobody is gonna save those ranches up by the Red River. Why, even the folks down here have Comanche trouble, let alone way up there and on their lonesome. I've heard of Buffalo Hump and five hundred warriors riding a thousand miles to go on a raid. That's some serious warriors who would go that far to kill trespassers. I'm afraid your ranch didn't stand a chance. Like I told ya before, Indians don't take kindly to folks stealin' their land."

"How are they gonna take to us? You know—you two being from the South and all."

"The war is over, Benji," Malvo said as he pushed back his hat, showing his green eyes and smiling a mouthful of teeth. "Most of us are all fought out. Some of these cavalry boys didn't even see action. There wasn't so much fighting here in Texas, not like in Eastern Louisiana. I heard the Texas Rangers were busy the whole-time fighting Apache and Comanche, though."

"You never know," Chito-Ochi said. "Sometimes you'll get the odd Northerner that still hates men like us, but we are in the South now, so there are more of us than there are of them. Most people we have met after the war are peaceful, except for a few that have gone bad. There is no point in dying for a lost cause."

"Apache *and* Comanche? And who are those who have gone bad?"

"And Kiowa, Tonkawa, Karankawa, and Tano-Tigua Indians, too," Chito-Ochi replied. "Then there is a scattering of the tribes from across the country like me who wander around looking for work."

"Some of the soldiers did too much killin'," Malvo said. "When they returned home, it was to burned out homes and cities. The war devastated the South. More than a few of those very soldiers turned into outlaws. Heck, I doubt they knew how to do anything else but fight anyway. Some were in the war and were not much older than you."

"What kind of work do you and Malvo do?"

I finally found the courage to ask the question I wanted answered from the moment I met these two strange men. I hadn't asked before because I was afraid of the answer. Now, it was too late to take back the question, and it seemed like they were taking forever to answer.

The men accompanying me locked eyes and shrugged.

"We run down bad men and bring them to justice,

at least when we can," Malvo slowly began, watching my face carefully. "Now, don't get me wrong. We ain't as nefarious as bounty hunters, but if the law is overwhelmed and they need help, we give our assistance for a price. We all gotta make a living somehow. The only way I know is with my guns and Chito-Ochi by tracking men. That's what we're best at. Right or wrong, the war made us who we are, much like that Comanche attack is making you who you're gonna be."

"Dying doesn't seem to be much of a way to make a living. It sounds mighty dangerous to me."

That night we bivouacked in a mountain pass. We could see the firelights of the army camp in the distance. The following day, we rode toward the army patrol's right flank. That was when the leader saw us out of the corner of his eye. We saw their dust cloud in the distance, as they pulled to stop.

"It looks like they're waitin' for us." Malvo grinned. "We don't wanna disappoint 'em and keep 'em waiting. Let's go, girls." He looked at me and wiggled his eyebrows.

We rode the last stretch of land between the soldiers and us, finally bumping our horses down two hundred yards out. Malvo led the way as he slowly walked his horse toward the officer. When we pulled up to the army patrol, Malvo and Chito-Ochi doffed their hats, and I followed suit. I noticed the blue uniforms and wondered what Malvo would do. He wore no hint of Confederate tags or badges, but he talked in a strong southern drawl and wasn't shy about who he was. Hopefully, there wouldn't be any trouble.

We already had enough on our hands. Hopefully, nobody talked about politics and wars this far west. Still, my pa always said there were still some hostile feelings between the Northerners and the Southerners. This soldier may be one and the same. I know my father never forgot, like he claimed to have. I could see it in his eyes whenever he talked to an ex-soldier from the South.

I just hoped my new friends didn't take a job helping the army before we got to a safe town. Despite what they said, I thought I might like El Paso enough to stay. Even though logic said to consider their line of work, my heart said this wasn't for me. I guess we would have to wait and see how it panned out.

It's not like I don't care for Malvo and Chito-Ochi, especially the Choctaw Indian. He treated me like an equal, whereas Malvo still treated me like a teenager—not quite like a boy, but not like a man, either.

I didn't begrudge him for it because I was pretty much a boy anyway, but I was dying to become a man as fast as possible. Whenever I thought I was there, I did something stupid that made my friends moan. If I wanted Malvo's respect, I would have to learn more and quicker.

Maybe when we get to El Paso, the town sheriff would have something easy for them to do, and I could tag along and learn something other than how to take care of horses. Then again, like most teenagers, I reckon I daydreamed too much.

From what I heard, I got the feeling that being a cowboy was low on the ladder in the West. Cowboys were paid three dollars a day all day long, but men skilled with guns and willing to make wrongs right made a lot more than that.

I wanted to ask Malvo how much money they made, but I knew that was a step too far. I didn't want to embarrass myself when he told me no. For now, the only thing I could say I knew how to do was work with cattle, but I heard half of the men in Texas were cowboys. That would make for some stiff competition.

Maybe if I needed to learn a new trade, now was the time before I got too old to pick and choose. I wonder what my pa would have thought if he could hear me now. I doubt he would think much of it, but his plan didn't work out at all. It got his family killed. Home-steading wasn't for me anymore, that much I was sure of. Maybe being a cowboy for the rest of my life wasn't either.

At this point, I was too confused to make a conscious decision. Perhaps I would head north with a big cattle drive all the way to Wyoming. I reckon a little breeze would push me in just about any direction.

"Have you men seen any thieves along the trail?" the chubby lieutenant asked as he scratched his graying whiskers. "Bentley's the name. And yours, mister?"

Obviously, he was utterly ignoring Chito-Ochi, and I saw that Malvo didn't like it. The officer sounded like the Northerner my father was talking about, and he had twenty men with him. I knew as soon as Malvo opened his mouth, things would begin to go south.

"My name is Malvo Tanner, and these are my friends, Chito-Ochi and Benji Willow."

"Where are you men going?" Lieutenant Bentley asked. "I see you've got extra horses. I could use a few new mounts myself."

"The horses ain't for sale," Malvo growled.

For a moment, I thought he was going to bite the soldier.

"You let me decide what's for sale and not, Johnny Reb," Bentley spat, then looked over his shoulder and back. He smiled sardonically.

"I said, our horses ain't for sale, mister," Malvo whispered just loud enough for the lieutenant to hear.

"You haven't answered my question yet, either," Bentley said. "Have you seen any thieves around? Or maybe you three are thieves I'm looking for."

When Malvo turned his eyes on the lieutenant, I could see him flinch. I wondered if he just saw those tombstones in there that I had seen before. Tanner drummed his fingers on his pistol grips, his fingernails clicking on the bone handles.

Tanner leaned closer to the officer and whispered, "Good or bad, it doesn't matter which way it goes. You're gonna be the first one to die. I might not get anybody else, but I'll get you, fatso. I didn't come here to start trouble. We're just passing through, but if you wanna stay here for good, make a move, and I'll see that they bury you, right here and now. It doesn't matter to me none. I died a long time ago, back in the war."

I was almost as shocked as the officer by what

Malvo said—especially the tone of his voice. It sounded like it came from the depths of hell. I was surprised the soldier didn't turn around and run. I don't think I've ever heard a man so scary sounding. When I looked down, my fingers were shaking. I had to grab one hand in the other to make them stop. I looked around, but everybody was looking at my White friend. They seemed to have forgotten about the Choctaw and me. They were all focused on the man with the guns.

"That's what I thought," Malvo said, now smiling as if nothing happened. "You'll find one of your thieves back a couple of days' ride, shot in the heart. If you find our camp, you'll find him in the bushes where I dragged him. He tried to rob us when the youngin was keepin' guard, and I killed him when he came at us with a gun."

Lieutenant Bentley nodded, his mouth a gash. I could tell he was as angry as the dickens, but I also saw the shock on his face. Now, I'm sure he saw what I did.

"Very well, sir," Bentley said, tipping his hat. He wheeled his horse and raced off with his patrol toward the dead thief.

"Why didn't that officer have his soldiers shoot us?" I asked Chito-Ochi when I had him alone. "It was getting pretty sketchy there for a spell."

"Malvo is smart and didn't threaten him loud enough for his soldiers to hear. Then, he would have forced him into action for honor's sake. The officer knew he was looking at a bullet for his efforts. Tanner knew he wasn't a stupid man, although he was arrogant and on the verge of insulting. I've seen him do bad things to men for less. But that was back in the war."

eleven
el paso, texas

I turned and looked at Malvo. The Choctaw Indian had disappeared again sometime last night. Then, I swung my eyes down-country and across the basin. The wind moaned, and a clutch of oak leaves scuttled across my feet. We saw the sun rise over a jagged rim of the earth to the east, making it flare behind the mountains.

"Don't just stand there like noon half-struck." Malvo grinned. "Let's get moving. Today, we can skip breakfast and eat hardtack and stale biscuits on the way. If we press the horses, we'll hit El Paso before dark."

I hung my canteen over the saddle horn, swung into my worn saddle, and clucked him forward. The horses' hooves clapped against the hard ground. I rocked back and forth, making the leather squeak. Malvo led the way, with me taking up the rear with the spare horses. My paint turned his head to bite me, but I slapped his face with my reins.

Acorn woodpeckers hammered on loblolly trees, emitting the smell of citrus as rock squirrels scampered from the ground and into the limbs above and out of sight, alarmed by the presence of humans.

We were trotting across a plain when we saw another horseman in the distance, maybe as far as a mile away. After a while, I could see the rider walking his horse, but the animal didn't seem right. When he stopped, it stood on three legs.

When we could finally make out who it was, I saw that the Choctaw and his horse had come up lame. We gigged our mounts into a gallop and rode toward our Indian friend. Behind us trailed three spare horses. In minutes, we pulled up before him and his limping animal.

"Howdy. Where've you been? I'm pretty good with horses. I grew up on a ranch, ya know."

I dropped down, walked over, drew up the horse's leg, and looked at the hoof's frog. It was split and bloody. Chata's animal quivered when I touched the sore hoof. I looked up and shook my head.

"That looks like a hard stretch of land ahead," Malvo said. "I doubt that horse is gonna make the cross. Heck, it might be a challenge for *us*."

"A desert?" Chito-Ochi said. "That doesn't mean anything to Indians. We've been here for thousands of years. This is the home of many tribes. We do not fear our backyard."

"El Paso has been around for a long time, too." Malvo smiled. "Some say it was founded as early as 1680 when it belonged to Spain. Indians aren't the only folks who live around here."

We set out walking our six horses, but the injured

animal continued stopping, sometimes not budging for minutes. Now I see why having a spare ride with us was always good. It was easy for one to come up lame. Still, I was surprised when I heard the gunshot. I looked back, and the Indian stood above the lifeless form.

The hot wind bore stinging bits of sand and grit. It peppered my face, but Malvo and Chito-Ochi didn't seem to notice and pushed on. I rode behind them like I didn't feel my burning cheeks. Desert chaff raced along the ground with migrant sands. As the wind continued to blow in minutes, our tracks disappeared behind us. The stiff breeze never seemed to cease. My horses' eyelashes were thatched with sand.

After days of riding, my ropy blond locks hung below my ears. I pushed back my hair and held it in place with my hat. I even had the shadow of a mustache and a few tiny patches of hair on my chin. I wasn't even old enough to grow a beard.

When Chito-Ochi disappeared again, I was initially puzzled because he had just returned. I looked at the sky—the sun said it was noon. I used the flat of my hand to shade my eyes as I gazed into the distance.

We suddenly noticed the dust cloud on the horizon. I looked back at Malvo, turned, and nudged my horse on, nodding. I remembered what Tanner had said about only riding with one horse and how dangerous it was. It turned out he was right.

We could smell the smoke of pinewood fires before we saw the city. It was Chito-Ochi who noticed it first. I've never seen a man with a nose like a bloodhound before. I could see the shapes of the mud buildings in the distance. People, like little ants, moved up and down streets. It looked as busy as a bee's hive.

"Is that El Paso?"

"It sure is," Malvo replied, grinning.

"It doesn't look like much, does it—all low and the color of dirt."

"Those are adobe buildings like the Mexicans make," Chito-Ochi said. "They don't look very pretty, but they are cool in the summer, and the fat walls are warm in the winter. Some are three feet thick. The Mexicans used to own this land, and before them, the Spanish."

Even before we entered town, I could hear the vendors cry out in the distance. Excitement replaced paranoia as soon we rode onto the main drag. It was alive with people. I hadn't seen so many people in years, which left me a little giddy. I saw shops scattered across town.

Cowboys raced their horses up and down the streets. They made up half the people I saw. Pretty women strolled down the boardwalk with umbrellas in their hands to ward off the sun. Their white faces shone under fancy bonnets. They ignored the looks and comments from the buckaroos. They acted like they weren't even there.

We rode through a plaza thronged with buckboard wagons and store goods stacked high on the boardwalk. Texans, Mexicans, and the odd Indian filled the streets. Two Indian army scouts stood by a building with their hands locked around the shafts of six-foot spears.

As we rode down the main street, we passed a high

adobe wall that said 'Jail' on one side and 'Sheriff's Office' on the other. Heavy timber doors barred the entrance. Broken glass was embedded on the top of the walls.

Noise flowed from small gaming houses. Piano music floated in the air from three saloons as though they were competing to see who played the loudest. I looked at the sun and it said seven. Soon, it would set. We had made it just in time. The cobbler, blacksmith, hatmaker, and others had their own small shops or stalls of adobe mud.

The church bell rang as a cloud of bats returned to their roost in the rafters. Kids with dogs sat on mud stoops and stared at the people passing by. My head swiveled on my neck like a spring doll. There were exciting things to see everywhere I looked.

Malvo and Chito-Ochi appeared to know precisely where they were going. Before I knew it, we tied our horses to the hitching rail in front of a large bar and dance hall. Boot heels hammered the porch, and the batwing doors whooshed when we entered.

When we walked into the Palace Saloon, men stood sideways at the bar with thumbs in their belts. A White man in the corner shook a rueful head and sipped his drink as he stared at Malvo and muttered. I shot a glance at him, but he didn't seem to notice, even though I knew he did. As far as I could see, he didn't miss a thing.

I could hear the warm wind blowing, and outside, I saw an enshadowed dark had fallen through the bar's windows. Somber and silent, Malvo appeared to be on a mission. He ordered a bottle of whiskey and three glasses.

"Not for me, Malvo. I don't think whiskey and me get along too good. Last time I felt ill for two days."

Malvo nodded and poured two drinks. They touched glasses and began to pass the night away, sitting there without a word as they went through the whole bottle. They drank on as the wind blew down the street and stars hung low overhead. I learned my lesson last time. With only two drinks, my head hurt so bad I thought it would burst.

We stayed until the ladies of the night and faro players were gone, and only the man sweeping the clay floor remained. At the back of the room, burned-blackened strips of anonymous meat were sizzling on a fire.

"It's hardly worth gettin' a place to sleep when I reckon it'll be dawn within the hour," Malvo said.

"We can stay in the stables for a nickel each," Chito-Ochi replied.

The roosters among the grapevines began to stir, and the first cock-a-doodle-doo broke the morning silence. This was my first time staying up all night in a saloon. The way they went after that bottle of whiskey made me believe maybe they hadn't been in a town for a long time. The last city I was in was when I was only ten.

The liveryman let us sleep in a stable, so I grabbed a pitchfork and forked hay to make a soft bed for us each. I was so tired I didn't care where I slept, and I suspected Malvo and Chito-Ochi had drunk enough to sleep sitting up. The last coyotes sang in the distance before they went out to start their nightly hunt.

I lay in the hay with my revolver on my chest and my hand wrapped around the grip—the six-gun capital of the world. The words made me wonder what would happen next. Just before I fell asleep, I gave a long, pneumatic sigh. For just a few hours, I would be at peace and asleep. We nestled like mice in the bed of hay.

twelve
staying behind

Soft voices in front of the livery woke me up. The first dusting of light crept across El Paso. Roosters cock-a-doodle-dooed somewhere nearby. I sat up, wondering what was going on. I rubbed my eyes with the heels of my hands and pushed myself out of the hay. The stable smelled of alfalfa. Particles of straw floated in the air where the light came in the open window.

When I walked out the stable door, I saw Malvo, Chito-Ochi, and a man with a badge. The owner was sitting against the barn on a bale of hay. Henry, the liveryman, appeared to mind his own business while the three men whispered in a huddle. The sheriff turned and glanced my way for a second.

Malvo's eyes followed his, but turned back, expressionless. Nobody offered to introduce me, so I sat down on the hay bale with the old farrier. We waited silently with questioning faces.

When they finished talking, Malvo and Chito-Ochi

turned toward the stables as the man with a star stormed off. Both their faces were dead serious.

"Work calls, Benji," Malvo said. "Are ya coming with us? Be forewarned; this ain't gonna be no stroll in the park."

"Whatcha gonna do—where ya gonna go?"

"What's the matter?" Malvo replied. "Work is work. That's not too hard to understand. So, are you coming or not?"

Malvo removed his hat and raked his long fingers through his shoulder-length hair, waiting for my answer. Chito-Ochi stood silently, finally raising an eyebrow.

I bunched up my lips and shrugged. My arms hung limp by my side. "I don't think I'm up to chasing bad guys yet. I'm afraid I've got to bow out."

I tried to keep a serious voice but noticed a hint of desperation. I looked at my boots and, with my toe, dug a little hole in the dirt.

A dark vein in Malvo's temple pulsed like a fuse, and his mouth formed a hard line. He forked his hat back with his thumb. The print of his hatband lay on his forehead like a white tattoo. He nodded, and they turned to get their horses.

Henry Hill craned his head to one side, pinched his nose with thumb and finger, and blew twin strings of snot onto the dirt. He wiped his fingers on his cotton shirt.

When they returned, Malvo said, "Look after the boy for me while we're gone."

The livery owner nodded and then spat in the dirt

at his feet. "Yeah, he can stay here for a spell, but I don't adopt kids. Just keep that in mind. I ain't an orphanage."

Malvo looked at the boy and saw the comment cut him to the quick. He wondered if the young man would man up or sweep saloons in El Paso for a living. There were already too many cowboys, and he knew when the railroads made it this far south, half the buckaroos in the county would be out of a job. He had seen the same thing happen in Kansas City back in 1865.

In minutes, they were storming out of the stable corral and racing down the street, and a wake of dust followed hammering hooves. They shot off like bullets. People stopped and stared until their images became smaller at the end of the street, then vanished beyond the crowd.

Then, they wheeled their horses and stormed away. After the men rode out, all that was left was hovering dust on the way out of town.

"Did they say where they were they're going? Or what they were up to? Maybe who they were looking for? I bet it was a dangerous outlaw."

"They never say where they're going," Henry replied as he stood. "Sometimes, they leave and don't return for half a year. Malvo's like that."

I don't know why I didn't expect it. It seemed to creep up on me, and before I knew it, I was alone—the precise thing I didn't want. Sure, El Paso was full of people, but I didn't trust them farther than I could throw them. Not even Henry, and Malvo had left me in his care.

I heard the calls of birds from the trees, the clink of harnesses, and shuffling horses as they gently cropped. The smell of charcoal and horses rode on puffs of air.

"I'll be back in a while."

I walked across the street toward the saloon closest to the livery on the edge of town. Henry told me he was going to put me to work, though. I could see he expected me to work for my room and board. That was fine with me because it kept my mind busy. My future was too dim and I didn't want to think about it.

I wondered what Malvo and Chito-Ochi were up to. I even wondered if they would return, and I still didn't know how I felt about that, either. Would it be a good thing, or would it be the worst mistake of my life?

In the chapel was an old Spanish bell, sea-green with age. It hung from a pole between two dolmen and rang every hour. I could imagine an old priest pulling the bell and being swept off his feet as the rope soared before dropping down again. The chapel walls were tall.

When I walked into the saloon, it reeked of sweat and wood smoke.

"Have ya got any 'bacca?" the Black man with the broom at the door asked with hopeful eyes.

"I'm sorry, but I don't smoke or chew, mister. My pa reckoned I was too young."

I made my way to the bar and a bowl of oatmeal. The barman pulled a gallon bottle of molasses from under the counter and let me have all I wanted. I put a little splash of milk and topped it with ground cinnamon. The second bowl finally filled my ever-hungry belly.

I decided I didn't want to stay in the smelly, smoky room any longer and turned toward the batwing doors. When I pushed my way out, I saw a girl skipping down the street, leading a horse as she sang something in a language I had never heard. I had no idea where she was from, but she sure was pretty.

There was something pleasing and pure in the young girl's eyes—especially when she suddenly smiled. She grabbed the horse by the reins and boldly walked it up to the porch. She blinked, and there was certainty in her gaze. When she passed me, she leaned closer to whisper in my ear. I drew in a sudden breath.

Her eyes widened, and she whispered huskily, "I like you. Do you like me?" Then she turned and ran away with her horse clopping behind her.

I didn't even catch her name, but I was more interested than ever in a girl. I didn't even know why. Maybe I *was* turning into a man. My palms were wet, and I broke out in a sweat. I sat there staring blankly into space for the longest time.

It was like I had forgotten where I was, and all it took was a whisper from a young girl who was not much older than me. I pressed my lips into a tight smile as my heart rate flew off the charts.

Henry, the liveryman, was spying from across the street. When she left, he cackled with delight. His laugh echoed down the street.

When I walked over, he said, "It looks like you've

taken a fancy to Ben's daughter and her to you. He owns the hardware store."

"What's her name?"

"Miranda," Henry replied, grinning, showing his missing front tooth. "Miranda Frank."

"That's not an American name, is it, Mr. Hill?"

"No, Miranda is Mexican," Henry replied. "The Apache killed her folks and kidnapped her, and Mr. and Mrs. Frank decided to adopt her once she was rescued."

"How did she get away from the Apache?"

"Some good men saved her, but the Franks ain't talkin'. They said the girl had already been through too much, so most folks let the poor young lady be. Me, I have my suspicions, but I don't gossip. Time will tell. Everything comes out in the end." Henry cackled with delight while my neck burned and got as red as a tomato.

When I returned to town, it was in the wee hours of the morning. The wide clearing was illuminated by orange-glowing windows. I could see a few people sitting around tables inside, but not like the earlier crowd. The yellow glow of kerosene lanterns reflected in the slightly steamed glass. Noise floated out of cracked windows.

I pushed my way back into the saloon, and at this early hour, it was quiet. I walked up to the bar and tapped on the counter with one of my dimes.

"A glass of cold milk, please."

The barman snickered, but he knew I was with Malvo. He smiled and brought me a mug full of white liquid. I put it to my lips and chugged. I didn't stop until I had finished half. I smacked my lips, and the man behind the bar smiled and turned to tend to the rest of his clients.

Suddenly, I found a man before me crouched, ready to lunge. He had a big knife in his hand and was eyeing my dimes. His clothes were in rags, and his boots had holes, but I didn't feel sorry for him. He reeked of cheap whiskey. He was a drunk looking to use my money to pay for his next bottle.

For a second, I froze. Then I looked down at my Colt Walker, and my lips curled. At first, the ornery fella thought he was dealing with a boy, but he suddenly realized he was facing a man, and he might be dangerous. I wrapped my hand around the cross-draw grip, one finger at a time until it formed a white-knuckled fist. I stared the thieving bum hard in the eyes.

"I don't remember orderin' stupid with my breakfast."

Suddenly, all that resolve I saw in his eyes a moment earlier dissolved, and he couldn't take his gaze off my big revolver.

"You can go now, thief. Bring me another glass of milk, please, barkeep."

I wiped the white mustache off my upper lip with the back of my hand.

"You wouldn't have shot that poor bum, would ya? I'm Billy, and this is my saloon. You seem a mite young to be carrying such a big gun."

"After what I've been through, I should be carrying my Winchester, too. The Comanche attacked me, and scalped and murdered my parents and twin brother. I've been ambushed by Indians, threatened by soldiers, and now a bum tries to rob me. I don't think so."

Billy's eyes popped when he heard my story.

"Excuse me, sir. Don't worry. I don't plan on shooting anybody or making trouble. I just showed him my gun, that's all. I thought it was funny when a thief brought a knife to a gunfight."

"Now that you put it that way, it is humorous. He's a barfly. I'll have a word with him, but I doubt he will come close to you again. When I saw your eyes, I thought you were gonna shoot him."

"How much do I owe you for the milk?"

"Here, have another one on me," Billy said. "It's good to see such a young man stand up for himself. There are a lot of bullies this far west, and you're gonna need all the grit you can muster. Some of those fellas from the war still have a chip on their shoulders. But I saw you riding with Malvo Tanner. I doubt you're a daisy if you're friends with him."

"Why do you say that? Malvo and Chito-Ochi saved my life up on the Red River. I rode down to El Paso with them, but I don't know what I'll do now— ride with Malvo or go back to working as a cowhand?"

"Cowboy life is mighty hard; I know firsthand, but you'll never be able to afford a girl like Miranda if you only make a hundred dollars a month," Billy said. "That's just enough to survive with a bit of tobacco and a couple of beers. Most boys think it's a lot of money when they get paid to herd cattle to Wyoming, but they don't consider all the time and hazards.

"Once they're there, they have to ride all the way back. That's why I picked tending bar. It's not all that safe in a town like El Paso, but it doesn't hold a light to riding the line all on your lonesome, waiting for a bunch of rustlers to kill you and steal the cattle."

As usual, my mind was clouded and too confused to know what to do. It was a heck of a big decision to make if it was to be for life.

After talking to Billy, I'm sure I don't want to spend the rest of my life in a saddle, chasing longhorns. I could work with horses if I could get the confidence of a rancher. I'm good at breaking wild strays. That was part of my job on our ranch. Then again, it probably didn't pay enough to have a home a girl like Miranda would expect.

I was surprised when I realized that I was thinking about Miranda again. I was obviously smitten by the girl. Her black hair seemed almost blue and matched her eyes. Her face was so beautiful that when I thought about her, my heart skipped a beat.

Later that night, as I lay in my hay bed, I wondered where my new friends were. Maybe I should have gone with them. It might have been a mistake not to go. It could be that they never invited me again or didn't return for six months, if ever. Times seemed unsure in Texas. Henry said that sometimes they would disappear for half a year.

thirteen
the job

"We better hurry," Chito-Ochi said. "We are wasting daylight standing here."

"I hear you. We're runnin' against the clock," Malvo said, wheeling his nervous horse around. It sidestepped and crow-hopped at first, but Tanner wrestled him under control.

"Do you think we'll catch up with them in time?" Malvo asked.

"We better. If not, there are going to be some innocent people sold into slavery," Chito-Ochi said. "They will probably end up some rich Mexican's slaves."

"If these men are scalpers like Sheriff Cassidy said, I wouldn't put nothin' past them. We're lucky they spotted them only a few hours ago, so they won't know we're chasing them. If we can catch them by surprise, we might save the captives in time. One way or another, whoever's responsible is heading for jail and probably a noose shortly after."

"That's not our problem," Malvo said. "Our job is delivering them, to face the music."

Two men leading two spare horses rode at a long gallop out of El Paso, heading west. The New Mexican border was only nine miles away. Once they crossed the state line, they would be in another jurisdiction. That was why the local sheriff didn't form a posse of deputized men and came to Malvo.

This was something that he couldn't broadcast. Sheriff Cassidy was dangerous, but he knew how to run the town and who to count on in a pinch. He couldn't go, so he sent somebody even better.

The Choctaw Indian and the White man met each other in the Confederate army. They both served through the entire war and had scars and medals to prove it.

Malvo Tanner didn't care where the bad guys ran. Considering who they were, he would follow them anywhere they went, no matter how far—all the way to Nevada if necessary.

Still, they knew the longer the clock ticked, the more probable that somebody would be sold or even killed if they thought the law was on their trail. The first thing they would do would be kill the witnesses and bury them where they couldn't be found, and they would be too late, so every minute counted.

"If the scalpers find out we are behind them, they will dump the children so they can make better time getting away," Chito-Ochi said.

The horses' lungs sounded like locomotives as they raced across the sunbaked land. Malvo's knees touched the long guns in his saddle's fenders. He fingered his revolvers in cross-draw holsters. He had to keep them handy because they may have to ride into a hot situation.

They would have to see where and when they caught up with the kidnappers, but catch them they would, or die trying. Tanner had already sworn an oath to God. There was no way he was going to let the victims die.

When Malvo was doing good for his fellow men, he tried not to feel righteous, but it wasn't easy. Some of the honor of success seeped in regardless of how noble he tried to be. That was one of the reasons he disliked the general population knowing the good things he and the Choctaw did. Then, these things would lose their value for them.

Every hour, Chito-Ochi dropped off his horse and inspected the tracks. He touched the edges with his fingers, picked up a handful of dirt, and smelled it like a dog. He looked up and stared into the distance, using the flat of his hand to shade his face.

Finally, he looked up at Malvo and said, "We'll catch them in half an hour or so, and they don't know we're behind them yet. Make sure you're ready. It's just about to come to a head."

First, they saw a dust cloud in the distance. They wheeled their horses toward higher ground, climbed a steep hillside, and jumped off at the top. Both men removed their Sharps rifles. They immediately set up their bipods and had their rifles in their hands, taking aim at the two leading men.

"You take the ones on the right, and I'll take the two on the left," Malvo whispered as he took a deep breath and let it out slowly, relaxing every muscle in his body.

Both rifles boomed simultaneously, and two men dropped off their mounts with heavy-caliber bullet holes in their backs. Blood sprayed their horses' heads. Two more shots rang out two seconds later. The racing horses fell, tumbling already dead. Then the riders slammed against the ground, dazed. The horses the captives rode spooked and bolted, but they stayed in sight.

Malvo and Chito-Ochi remounted, scrambled down the hill, and set their spurs. Their horses bolted like their tails were on fire. In seconds, Tanner was on top of the outlaws.

"Get the youngins!" Malvo shouted. "I'll take care of this sum."

Chito-Ochi raced down the runaway horse with two small children sitting terrified in the saddle. They were both shaking like leaves. They were no more than little kids. He shook his head at how bad men would stoop to such low and disgusting deeds.

He grabbed the horse's lead and wheeled for his business partner. This was more about doing the right thing than anything else. They were lucky this time, and nobody but two of the scalpers died. The other two wouldn't have long to live.

Chito-Ochi left the outlaws to Malvo and offered the small children pieces of sweet sugarcane to gain their confidence. Even though he was an Indian, they felt rather than saw his good intentions. It was a fact that this Indian was a strange man, but his heart was so big if he opened it to you, you felt it.

"The sheriff back in El Paso sent us to rescue you," the Indian said in a soothing voice. "Are you both all right? Did these bad men harm you? You don't have to worry now. You're with me and Malvo."

The children grabbed the cane sticks and stuck them in their mouths, chewing away and shaking their heads, yes and no. Despite their fear, the sweet treat was exactly what they needed. It distracted them for the time being.

"Let's get you two back to El Paso and safety," Chito-Ochi said. "Are you ready to ride, Malvo?"

"Let me tie these two dung birds up first. Come on and help me throw them over their saddles. We better scare up those two horses before we leave, too. We can bring the dead bodies back to El Paso. Benji is short a horse anyway. He can have one of theirs, and we'll leave the other in Henry's stables for when we need it."

"I was surprised he didn't want to come with us," Chito-Ochi said. "I thought he was ready. Maybe you're wrong, and he is not cut out for this kind of work."

"He's a smart boy. I wouldn't go if I wasn't told where I was going, either, even if it was with friends. He had a right to know, and next time, I plan to give it to him. But if he doesn't go on the second offer, I reckon he'll have to get a job on a ranch, cattle drive, or maybe Ben Frank at the hardware store will give him a job sweeping up. I must admit, it'll disappoint me if he passes on the opportunity. The young critter is already growing on me."

"Not everybody's like us. You know most people see us as bounty hunters."

"You know I don't consider us bounty hunters," Malvo snapped. Then he looked at his friend. His eyes said he was sorry. "You know what I mean. I've never chased a man on a poster unless innocent folks' lives were in danger. I prefer to prevent violence, when possible, rather than kill men for what they've done. That's the town sheriff's job. That's what Boon got hired for, and he does the job even if he is an angry man."

"He isn't angry around women." The Indian chuckled. "Then he is a gentleman, like Benji calls us."

"No, he's not. The women think he's a handsome fella. They like tall men—you know, the hero types. You know he has a dark side, too. He's been in a dozen gunfights, and some say two or three were questionable."

"I believe that is none of our business," Chito-Ochi said. "The elders of El Paso like him enough. Before Boon came to town, walking down the street was dangerous, especially for women and children, not to mention Indians, no matter what their tribe."

"I wouldn't give him a silver star just yet." Malvo snickered. "You just never know; one day, *we* might be at odds."

When they made their way back to town, they stopped by the hardware store to meet with Sheriff Cassidy and Ben Frank, one of the town's councilmen.

He would take charge of the children until they found a kind home to take them in.

There were a lot of orphaned children on the western plains. Luckily, there were enough good people out there to make homes for many of them. Hopefully, these two would find a nice family to adopt them too.

"The commonness of death in El Paso makes reference to it almost casual," Mr. Frank said, shaking his head. "They don't call it the six-gun capital of the West for nothing."

"I'm afraid that in El Paso, funerals have become a monotonous regularity," Malvo replied. "Why, I reckon in a few years, the town will have the biggest Boot Hill in America."

"That's true enough," Ben Frank replied. "At the way things are going, one day we might kill each other off, and El Paso will become a ghost town."

"There is little chance of that," Chito-Ochi said. "El Paso has been here for two hundred years."

"What did you do with those two young children?" Missus Frank asked. "You know we can always take one or two more. Miranda would love to have a younger brother and sister."

"It's arranged, dear," Ben said. "They are going to your sister, Marge."

"Is this the same agreement as last time?" Malvo asked. "This stays a secret, just like Miranda, right?"

"Why won't you take the credit for saving them?" Missus Frank asked. "It'll make a lot of people happy. You are good men." She turned and looked at the Choctaw Indian. "Both of you."

"It'd be bad for business, ma'am," Malvo replied. "If folks think we are goin' soft, they won't believe we're up to the job anymore."

"Here, take this," Ben Frank said as he opened his palm. Five double silver eagles lay in his open hand. "It's not much for risking your lives, but you should be paid something."

Malvo shook his head and said, "We don't take money to save children, Ben. You know that."

"I don't see why not," Frank replied.

"Doin' good deeds is our pass to the pearly gates when we die." Malvo smiled. "If we took money for savin' children, those gates might be closed when we get there. You keep your coins, Ben. With that young daughter of yours, you're going to need 'em. It looks like she'll grow up to be a beauty."

"I'll arrange for someone reliable to take the children over to your kin, darlin'. They'll have a happy family there. I don't think Miranda would like the competition anyway. She's mighty spoiled, ya know. Everything is peaceful here at home, and I'd like to keep it that way."

When they walked their horses into the livery corral, I was pitching hay into all the stables. I looked up when I heard horses' hooves approaching. My eyes twinkled when I saw my friends. They *did* make it back, and not six months later. I sighed with a breath of relief.

I'd been working up the nerve to ask Malvo where they'd been and what they'd done. I knew he probably wouldn't tell me—he was like that sometimes. But I couldn't contain myself. I had to know, especially if I wanted to decide if I would follow in his footsteps or not. At least I needed to know what he expected of me. He couldn't ask me to walk into a dangerous situation blindly. Still, I had no intention of saying no again.

"Tell me, Malvo, what did you two just do? I see that smug, satisfied look on your face. If you want to help me decide what I'm going to do for a living in the future, a lot rides on what you've got to say."

"We saved a boy and a girl from scalpers. Two of the men that did it are sitting in the sheriff's jail right now. The other two are at the funeral parlor, waiting for burial up on Boot Hill in an unmarked grave. People don't take kindly to bad men stealing young children, so I doubt they'll see the inside of a prison. More than likely, they'll end up on the top of a gallows swinging by the end of a rope."

When the truth settled in about the kidnapped children's rescue, my eyes spread, and my heart began to beat nervously as an anxiousness came over me, leaving me silent. I blinked like a bird.

"You?" I whispered, and then I looked at Chito-Ochi. "And you?"

"That's what Chito-Ochi and I do, son," Malvo said. "We save people, when possible, who are in dire straits. Sometimes, the jobs are a little different, but that's the gist of it all. Sometimes, we get paid for it, and sometimes, we don't. It was best you didn't ride along this time because this time, we didn't make a dime. You *do* want to make some money to buy yourself some new clothes before you begin to spark and court one of these pretty girls in town, don't cha?"

Back in the jail, both kids were sobbing from the shock and happy with the relief that they were freed. For some men, sometimes that was reward enough. This little girl's and boy's minds surpassed fear, worry, and dread. They continued to look completely confused and stared blankly. All Malvo could do was hope they snapped out of it. Sometimes, the young ones saw too much, and their minds went.

"I reckon we got those two little ones in the nick of time." Malvo smiled. "All they need now is some tender loving care, and they'll survive just like the rest of us."

"Gosh, who would have ever thought? Maybe I *do* want to be like you and Chito-Ochi. Like our Choctaw friend says, things are already planned out anyway. Maybe meeting you two *was* my destiny."

fourteen
first romance

Some people told me your first romance was always the best. I wondered why the first couldn't be the last, too. Since Malvo and Chito-Ochi returned, I stopped fretting about them and began worrying about Miranda. I wondered if she still liked me as much as I liked her or if she only wanted to be friends. I was a fourteen-year-old trying to court and spark a girl a couple of years my elder. Then again, with my height, I looked older, too.

I nearly stumbled and fell every time I saw her in the street. When she talked to me, I suddenly felt too stupid to speak all, to the amusement of Malvo and friends. They all seemed to enjoy seeing me put my foot in my mouth time and again.

Miranda laughed, too, but that was different. Whatever she did, I didn't mind because I saw she was happy. She strangely found my fumbles and moments of puzzlement extremely funny and showed it by her laughter.

Some days, I would wander around the tailor's

shop to see how much new clothes cost. I also needed new boots and a hat. When I found out how much money I needed, I was shocked. If I wanted to court the hardware store owner's daughter, I had to dress better than I did.

At night, while I lay in the hay staring at the ceiling, I would daydream about all the things I desired. Most were to look good for Miranda. I wondered what she would say if I asked her to be my girl. I'm sure it was too soon, especially since, technically, I was still out of work. I didn't want her to think I was a bum, nor could I ask her father permission to stroll about town if I dressed like a rag-picker.

It wasn't my fault my family was poor, but if you wanted a woman, you had to have something to offer. Me, as I was, wouldn't cut it. It was better if I continued to be friendly but refrained from doing anything about it until I could come courting dressed like a man and not a ranch rat. That meant I had to have a job, and any job wouldn't do. It had to be something I could call a proper wage. Only then could I start courting the girl I was crazy about.

I was working outside, helping Henry re-shoe a horse. I was impressed by his skills with animals. As soon as he touched their withers, they visibly calmed. Some said he was what they called a horse whisperer, whatever that was.

I'd never seen him whispering to horses, but he did seem to be able to talk to them with his hands. This one appeared to like it, especially when he scratched its muzzle and chin. I helped him out with the hoof pick and cleaned out the dirt, mud, rocks, and manure, always working from heel to toe.

We were finishing when Miranda came riding up to the hitching posts unannounced. She wore tight boy's britches and shiny new boots and seemed to bubble and bounce in the saddle. I noticed when she kicked her leg over the horn and gracefully slid to the ground. When she landed, her boots made little puffs of dust, and a light coating covered her boots.

"Hello, gentlemen," Miranda said as she stared openly at me. "What's the matter? Haven't you learned to speak yet, or is it just that you're dumb?"

She giggled when she said it. As usual, she put me off balance by making fun of me. Still, I couldn't resist.

"You know I'm not dumb," I huffed, dusting the dirt off my pants with my hat. The sunlight made my blond hair shine, and my green eyes sparkle.

Despite her joking manner, I saw the look in her eyes. I wondered what she saw in mine. We seemed to get lost in each other's stare for a moment, and we forgot where we were, and that Henry was standing right there beside us.

"When you two look at each other, you get all googly-eyed," Henry said, slapping his knee as he burst out laughing. "Excuse me, I'm gonna get some nails and nail nippers. I must be gettin' forgetful in my old age. Don't you run away now, Benji. I'll be back in a spell."

Henry winked at me when Miranda wasn't looking before he disappeared into the stables. His elbows jerked as he hobbled to the large wooden door. He had been badly wounded in the knee during the war and had walked with a limp ever since.

"Now that we're alone, don't you have anything to say?" Miranda asked. "I know you're clever. My father said so. I heard him talking to Fred, the cashier in the store."

"For some reason, I seem lost for words whenever I try to talk to you. I don't know what comes over me. If not, I'd charm you with my wit, but as soon as you get near, I forget all my clever things to say."

"So, you *do* have a crush on me," Miranda said, smiling. "I just knew it."

"Is that good or bad?" I didn't know what to think.

"It's good, silly. Can't you see how happy I am? Shush now about this. My father can't know about this until you have a job. You said you were looking for work, didn't you? He doesn't approve of lazy men, and I don't, either."

"I've already got something lined up, and it's supposed to pay pretty well."

"What is it? Come on, you *must* tell me." Miranda batted her eyelashes.

"Until it's a done deal, telling you any details wouldn't be gentlemanly."

I had to lie through my teeth. I still didn't know exactly what I would be doing anyway. I wondered what she and her father thought about Malvo Tanner and Chito-Ochi, the Choctaw Indian. I thought it better not to go into detail until I talked to my friends. The exact name of what they did escaped me, so I told a little fib.

Malvo had informed me loud and clear they weren't bounty hunters. So, what exactly did they do? I know they saved the two kids but didn't get paid for *that*. I wonder what it was like when they *got* paid.

"All right, I can wait, but when you get the job, you must tell me all about it." Miranda whispered like it was our little conspiracy. "I'm just happy you've found something suitable. Maybe if I introduce you to my father, he'll let us have a stroll around town one morning. I'm sixteen, you know. Where I'm from in Mexico, I would already be married and waiting for my first child. But I'm not in a rush, as long as I have a good-looking man waiting for me. How's that sound to you, Benji?"

Just the fact that she called me a man nearly knocked me over. The Mexican girl winked, and her smile grew into a grin as her white teeth flashed in the sunlight. I didn't know what kind of perfume she wore, but it knocked me out. It was nothing like the perfume women in cheap dresses wore in the town saloons. It was alluring without being overpowering, just enough to get my undivided attention.

Feral lovebirds chirped behind the stables. Buckboard wagon wheels rolled dust down the street as groups of cowboys trotted by. Some caught sight of Miranda and stared, but she didn't even notice. That surprised me because it made me happy. It seemed she only had eyes for me.

Miranda turned and blew me a kiss. My mind spun for a moment as I thought I almost felt it on my cheek.

Then just as fast as she arrived, she was gone again, leaving me more confused than ever.

"Sometimes women are just jealous of how simple a man's brain is," Henry said.

"How old are you, Henry?"

"I'm not exactly sure, but becoming old was the dumbest thing I've ever done."

fifteen
growing up

Malvo had disappeared early that morning before I got up, and Chito-Ochi had suddenly vanished the night before. One minute he was there, and the next, he wasn't. It happened so often that I hardly noticed the absence of the Choctaw, but Malvo I missed. Finding him gone made me nervous, even though I didn't know why.

After pulling on my boots, I slipped my suspenders over my shoulders and headed for the small kitchen at the back of the stables. I grabbed two cold biscuits, forked a peach from an open tin of fruit, and headed out front to see what Henry had for me to do. Maybe he would know where Malvo had gone. I checked, and his horse was still there.

When I walked into the sunlight, I was blinded for a moment as I chewed a mouthful. I looked up when somebody cleared their throat, and I squinted my eyes to see who it was.

"Well, are ya comin' this time or not?" Malvo asked

as he stared deep into my eyes. "I know ya got the grit. All ya have to do is get your head around the whole thing. I understand you're a mite young for such business but sometimes life throws us something that sets the course of our lives. I don't think ya wanna miss that. At least now ya know we ain't killers like you first thought."

"Why, I never even imagined such a thing."

I shouldn't lie about it, but now that I know they're honorable men, I'd feel bad if they believed I *had* thought they weren't honest.

"I only think the best of both of you. You're my only friends." This I said from my heart.

"How ya doin', Malvo?" Henry asked as he limped out to see if he couldn't hear some good gossip. He made it to the bale of hay and sat down, cupping his ear as he watched. A toothpick moved from one side of his mouth to the other.

Everything that went on in town, Henry knew about it. Of course, being the only livery in the city meant he knew every time somebody came and went and overheard everything they said. Henry Hill was a snoopy old cuss, but deep down inside, he was a decent man. It was buried under that grumpy façade of his.

"It is time you grabbed the bull by its horns, Benji," Chito-Ochi said, then he turned and whispered into my ear. I saw Malvo look at us funny. "Come along, Benji. I've never seen Malvo invite anybody to ride with us, and you might not get another chance. This is the second time and might be the last."

"What're you two whisperin' about?" Malvo asked

knowingly. He had ridden with the Indian for so long that they almost knew what each other thought. "I can smell the wood a-burnin'. If you can't make up your mind, you ain't ready anyway."

"I'm going with you, Malvo." I smiled. "I wouldn't miss it for the world. Today will be the first day of my new career. You can't feed a lady like Miranda on a cowboy's salary."

They both snickered. They knew I was young, but I didn't sit on my laurels like most. Now, it was time they found out if I had what it took to do their job. Malvo didn't believe you could put an age or a name on such work. He believed they were like some sort of lawmen without badges or politicians telling them what to do and not do. Sometimes, it was even up to them to decide what was right and what was wrong.

In an hour, we were saddled up and heading for New Mexico. Even though I said I wouldn't, I still hadn't asked them what we would do. I wanted to stay focused to ensure I didn't chicken out and did the right thing. Now that we were out of town, I believed asking was safe. I nudged my new horse and pulled up next to Malvo. Chito-Ochi had yet to appear.

"You know, I used to fancy myself in a Confederate officer's uniform festooned with medals, but that ship has long sailed port and won't be comin' back," Malvo said with dreamy eyes. "The wars are over, and we lost. Any respect we had during the conflict was stolen from us when we lost it, and it's taking a long time to recover. The spoils go to the victors, and the losers don't get squat."

I didn't know where all that came from, but I didn't think it was the right time to interrupt. I felt uncomfortable talkin' about the war with my family being Northerners and my pa fightin' for the Union. Even though that was a long time ago for me, for those who were there, it didn't seem so long at all. For them, it was almost like yesterday when they lost their homes and families to the conflict. The pain was still deep and raw. I could see it in Malvo's face.

Chito-Ochi wasn't as affected as his White friend. Maybe that was because he was working as he was now and wasn't politically invested. He was paid a wage just like the rest of the soldiers, but his job was tracking the enemy and ensuring they didn't walk into ambushes. Often, he disappeared for days on end, just like now. But he was a Choctaw before he was an American or Confederate. That much even I understood.

Once the war was over, he followed his best friend home and was welcomed with cold ashes and vanished loved ones. Some died, others fled, and no trace of them was left. They wandered for months, looking for some sign of Malvo's people.

All they found were angry soldiers and people from both sides. Texas was one of the only places not so affected, so they rode south like many Confederates. There, they knew they would be safe from angry officials, and maybe they could start a new life and forget the war.

Malvo went silent for a while. Then, just like always, Chito-Ochi appeared behind us. I didn't even hear his horse. I nearly jumped out of my skin when he tapped me on the shoulder, laughing. It seemed he got a kick out of sneaking up on White people. Or maybe he just liked to scare *me*.

"Where are we headed, and what're we going to do? I have my guns ready."

"Easy now with them pistols, Trigger. We're headed for Socorro, New Mexico," Malvo replied as he stared into the distance. He pulled his hat down low to help shade his eyes. "Boon is from there. He said somebody threatened a friend and wanted to kill her. We're to babysit a woman and fend off aggressors if they happen to show up. We get thirty dollars a day for the three of us. The minimum stint is ten days and twenty dollars a day if it takes longer. They get a discount for the added time. Is that all right with you, lady's man?"

"Babysitting is not one of my favorite jobs, but it is perfect for you to start, Benji," Chito-Ochi said. "It's not bad money, either. We stand to make a hundred dollars each for ten days of work and six days riding. Where else can you make that kind of money even if we do have to risk our lives?"

"Why do we get paid so much?" I watched the amused faces of my friends.

"When you're getting shot at, and you have to stand your ground and shoot back, you tell me if we're getting paid too much or too little, son." Malvo laughed. "That money also goes for the reputation. We've been fighting for over a decade, so we've become pretty good at it. That's something that you're going to have to earn."

"So, we're gonna protect a woman? That doesn't sound like a bad job. Is she pretty?"

"How would I know?" Malvo smiled. "You seem to have a one-track mind, young fella. When we're workin', you can forget about chasing skirts, boy. It's time to focus. What would happen if you wagged your jaw with the lady and the bad guys showed up? You'd be unprepared. Not being ready in this business could cost you yours and the lady's lives."

"With our luck, she will be eighty years old, have no teeth, and be deaf," Chito-Ochi said jokingly. "Old White women get grumpy—especially with Indians."

We rode until we saw Las Cruces, New Mexico, in the distance. The town was lit up with lights. It was one hundred and ninety miles to Socorro, and we wanted to get there within three days. That meant there was no time to stop and enjoy the city. Maybe we would have time when we returned.

That night, wolves raced around our camp. They were after the horses, but Malvo kept them at bay. When they ran past, he fired shots into the air to scare them off. When that didn't work, he aimed. The wolf yelped when the bullet hit. I didn't know if it was dead or alive, but the rest of the pack disappeared and didn't come back. I would have to wait until the morning to see what happened.

We slept like dogs in the sand that night until something black flapped beside me. At first light, a wrinkled face with vicious bare lips, a terrifying smile, and a blue beak looked at me. It twisted its neck, folding its wings over the dead wolf to drink its blood. More vultures circled low in the air, waiting for a safe moment. The bold buzzard looked at me defiantly as it tore at strings of meat.

I jumped to my feet. It scared the daylights out of me. When it startled and flew away, I could feel the air from its whooshing wings and saw its bloody beak when it soared, joining its friends. They continued to circle in the sky above us but now higher. It was only a matter of time before they would have their next meal as soon as we humans left.

"What is that dust cloud in the distance?" I pulled to a stop, concerned, wrinkling my brow.

It was the second day, and the sun baked the land as images wavered on the horizon. The constant breeze peppered my face with sand. Lizards sunbathed lazily on hot rocks. Only mesquite and cactus were visible. I looked at the sun: it was noon.

"Why, it's the Socorro to El Paso stage-coach," Malvo said. "Let's ride down there and wait for them to pass by. The horses could use an hour's rest."

"Is Mad-Dog Reeds still driving stagecoach-es?" Chito-Ochi asked.

Malvo pulled to a stop and stared through his spyglass. "That's Mad-Dog, all right. Let's go down and say howdy."

We broke into a gallop as we rode down a long slope of gravelly dirt. It crunched under our horses' hooves as they breathed heavily. My mouth was dry, my lips chapped, and my face sunburned.

When we got closer, I saw a wild-looking man with a long whip, cracking it over the heads of the racing team of horses. The stage driver at the reins had a white beard, and his white mop of hair was covered by a bullet-ridden hat. A cold pipe hung from his lips.

"Whoa, whoa, girls!" Mad-Dog yelled.

He booted the brake with his foot and wrapped the reins around the brake handle. When he turned to Malvo, he showed a toothless smile as mischief danced in his eyes.

"Whatcha doin' over *this* way, Malvo?" Mad-Dog asked. "Last we talked, you were headin' for California."

"He's been heading for California for years." Chito-Ochi chuckled. "We have good intentions, but something always comes up. We never seem to get past Arizona."

"Ya seen any trouble?" Malvo asked. "Are there any bands of Indians out there makin' a fuss?"

"No more than the odd Apache trying to steal something from White folks. Lucky for me, things have slowed down here for a spell. I hear it's worse with the Comanche up north in the Texas Hill Country."

"That it is. This here is our new man, Benji Willow," Malvo said.

Mad-Dog doffed his hat, and I tipped mine. His lips disappeared when he grinned, the edges touching his ears.

"You're a mite young to be huntin' down wicked men, ain't cha, son?" Mad-Dog asked.

"I don't think we're hunting down outlaws, sir. I think we're bodyguards for the moment."

"You must be the politest fella in New Mexico." Mad-Dog smiled. "Do ya know how to use that big gun of yours?"

I nodded, wondering if he was making fun of me. The man seemed to like to talk.

The passengers began to peek out the window with their eyes spread. Some of them opened curtains as they blinked against the sun. Sweat rolled down their faces, and their clothing stuck to their backs as the heat soured inside the confined wooden box.

"Is there trouble, driver?" a woman asked. "Are these men here to rob us? Is that an Indian?"

"No, no, and yes," Mad-Dog growled. He gave them a look that said don't bother me again.

The curtains suddenly closed, and not a word more was heard. The team of six horses shifted their hooves nervously, but the driver ignored everybody as he chatted with his friends.

"I'm doin' the round trip from home and back," Mad-Dog said. "As you can see, we have a lively crowd back in the coach. There are two dandies on the backseat, too, but they're so scared I haven't heard a peep from them all day. I hope they didn't fall off."

"You never change, Mad-Dog," Chito-Ochi said. "We must go and do our job."

"He's right, ya know," Malvo replied.

"Who ya off to save now?" the stage driver asked.

"Nobody in particular. We're supposed to stand guard for some friend of Boon Cassidy's."

"You say kin of the sheriff's?" the driver asked.

"Yeah—what is it you know that I don't, and I ain't going to like?" Malvo asked.

"Maude Granger." Mad-Dog grinned. "I betcha money it's something to do with her and that Spanish woman she's lookin' after. She's the only kinfolk I know of Boon Cassidy in Socorro. She's crazier than a rat in an outhouse, but the European woman is mighty fine to look at, although she's a bit young for you, you old dog."

"Driver!" the woman passenger dared complain again.

"Shush, woman. Can't you see us men are talkin'?" He cracked his whip for effect and turned back to his friends. "Now, where were we?"

"I can't stay all day and jaw-wag, pard," Malvo said. "We've got to get movin'. I hope you're not right about this woman. Then again, how much trouble could she be?"

"That'll be for you to find out, old buddy." The stage driver unwrapped the reins and slapped them across the horses' backs as he cracked his whip over their heads. "Come on, girls, gitty-up."

I could hear him cackle as the stagecoach quickly disappeared into its cloud of dust.

sixteen
socorro

On the third day, we saw the town. As we rode toward the setting sun, shades of red shot across the sky to the other side of the world, and the yellow disk began to vanish before my eyes. I saw the silhouettes of a string of wolves on a nearby ridge as their shadows stood long like black pencil marks. The town of Socorro lit up one light at a time, eventually making a yellow circle glow around the city.

"Is that it? Socorro, I mean?"

"Yes, it is. This town got discovered by the Spanish in 1598. It's been around for a long time," Malvo said. He seemed to know a lot about everything. "Socorro means help. It would be a good idea if you learned how to speak Spanish like my Choctaw friend and me. Workin' here down, it comes in handy if we have to ride south of the border, especially if you want to court and spark that young Mexican lady, Miranda. Lucky for me, I learned from a woman I was in love with. Maybe that will work for you."

"Do you know what love is?" the Indian asked.

"I probably wouldn't know if it hit me on the head, but I'm eager to learn. When I'm near Miranda, I get a funny feeling in my stomach, but then I get as stupid as a potato. Is that what love feels like?"

"I don't know myself. Love seems to have escaped me, but there's still hope." Chito-Ochi smiled.

"Strong feelings are hard to decipher at times," Malvo said as he got an unusual look in his eyes. "A young man might think he's feeling love when it's entirely something else."

"In the beginning of time, the Piro-speakers of the Teypana Pueblo lived here, in Socorro," Chito-Ochi said. "That was long before the Spanish Conquistadors arrived and conquered the entire South American continent. White men have been pushing us out of the way for much longer than you think."

"Yeah, but White men made it a proper town in 1844, so it's not all that old," Malvo said.

"The Mexicans' village has been here for two hundred fifty years," the Choctaw said.

For me, it was like having an encyclopedia at my fingertips. My new friends seemed to know a lot about the land where we lived. I'd only heard about places like Europe, which didn't interest me much.

But what happened in America during the Revolutionary and Civil Wars always got my attention, along with the explorers of the time. I often dreamed of being like Lewis and Clark. Maybe now I would have a chance to make a small mark on history.

It was just turning dark when we rode into town

with six horses clapping on the hard street of the main drag. The air smelled of charred wood, and the perpetual wake of dust followed us. We wheeled toward the town livery stables to have our animals tended to, fed, watered, and bedded down.

Once we finished there, we made a beeline for the town sheriff's office. Boon claimed he was his friend, but Malvo said Cassidy was prone to stretching the truth. Still, the lawman was good to have around if there was trouble. He could shoot as well with his left hand as his right and was rumored to have once been a gunfighter. Falsehood or truth—who was to say? At least he was impressive, even for a Texan sheriff.

To me, Socorro looked pretty much like El Paso, only smaller. Most of the buildings were mud brown. There was also a chapel in the town center with a brass bell high in the tower that rang every hour on the minute. Stray dogs barked behind the diners and bars, and music spilled out the windows of the dance halls. The setting sun gave a small respite from the daily heat.

"There's the sheriff's office, over there," Malvo said. "The word I got is he's guarding the woman there until we arrive, and then we'll stand guard at her place, I guess. I don't fancy spending much time in a jailhouse. To be honest, I ain't sure how this is going to work. We don't even know who's supposed to be after her. Boon said he would tell me before we left, but he didn't come through, which ain't so unusual with him. But the money's good and the job sounds easy enough."

"That's what worries me," Chito-Ochi said. "When things seem too easy, they usually become difficult. Still, making money is nice. We can only do so many jobs for free. A man must eat and have money for bullets and the odd necessity."

When we stopped in front of the jail, I dropped down, crossed the small porch, and looked in the window, cupping my hands around my eyes. Lamplight glowed through the glass, making my hair appear yellow.

"That's a good way to get shot, boy," Malvo said. He fingered his pistol grips, which seemed like a habit when he got a little nervous.

"Do you really think a sheriff's gonna shoot a kid? We can get away with more than you old guys can. Nobody thinks we're dangerous."

"There're some treacherous youngins in New Mexico," Malvo replied. "Hard country breeds hard men." He looked across the street. "Go over and save us a table before there's none left. We'll be right along as soon as we find out what's going on."

I must admit I was disappointed. I was anxious to see who this mysterious woman was. When I got inside the restaurant, a group of cowhands vacated a table beside the window. I was dressed the same as them.

Most of us had holes in the bottoms of our boots, and our shirt cuffs were frayed. Soon, I would be going shopping for new duds and a hat that wasn't so floppy and old. Maybe even some boots without holes in the soles. Mine were hand-me-downs from my pa.

As I waited and sipped on a glass of milk, I kept my eyes glued to the sheriff's office door. I could see silhouettes behind the window but couldn't make out anything else. Another stagecoach came roaring into the city, nearly running over a group of pedestrians.

As it rolled around the corner, it tipped onto two wheels for an instant, then righted itself and raced down the street. Dust spun around the wagon wheels. Even inside the diner, I could hear the driver holler.

Arrows protruded from all over the stage and into the luggage on top. A wounded shotgun guard lay hanging from the edge, precariously teetering, almost ready to drop. The wild-eyed driver jumped down and forgot to set the brake, and the carriage started to roll down the street on its own.

An arrow stuck out from the driver's arm and another from his leg. He took two steps and dropped to his knees, gritting his teeth in pain. A cowboy quickly climbed onto a horse and raced to the stage. He jumped onto the seat, booting the brake, and tied off the reins.

I sat and watched in horror as the stage door swung open, but somehow, the people inside appeared uninjured. Still, they stepped down wobbly-legged and as white as ghosts. Their survival must have been due to the skills of the bullwhacker.

Apparently, the Apache were almost as bad here as the Comanche in the north. I thought the whole town would gather and gawk, but half the people didn't seem very interested.

Maybe this wasn't as unusual here in New Mexico as I thought, but it shocked *me*. Then again, if the truth were known, I was still a little scared of hostile Indians, yet I knew it was something that I would soon have to overcome. We would undoubtedly run into some

Apache while I'm working with Malvo. He mentioned maybe going down to Mexico, and I've heard there they are as thick as ants.

Out of the corner of my eye, I saw movement on the jailhouse porch. It was Malvo, Chito-Ochi, and a man with a badge over his heart. They shook hands, and he turned and went back inside, ignoring the stage. I wondered what in the world happened and where the mystery woman was. Both men strode across the street for the diner. In two minutes, they were pushing their way through the door.

"What's happening? Where's the lady?"

Malvo and Chito-Ochi slid into their seats beside me, and at first, they seemed not to want to talk. I began to feel uncomfortable. Fortunately for me, they saw it and opened up.

"First things first," Malvo said. "Right now, we've got to eat. All of us are gonna have a long night tonight. I think it's gonna be a little more complicated than we thought. She's still in the sheriff's office. I figured we needed time for some grub to boost our energy, and then we could get down to work—that and several cups of coffee. We're all worn out from three days of hard riding. How are you holding up, Benji?"

"I'm just fine."

Complicated? I still didn't have any idea what was happening. But I knew better than to ask and kept my mouth shut. I was the inexperienced one in the group. Heck, I was only in my teens. Still, I noticed how I had beefed up over the last weeks, and I was already five feet ten. I guess I was going to be a tall man like Malvo and Boon.

For me, two men couldn't be more different. I quickly noticed how the personalities of the sheriff and my friend clashed somehow. One was a façade of niceness but when behind the curtain, I was sure there was a killer. Sure, Malvo appeared mean and hard, too, but inside, there was a good, honest man. I am beginning to believe that was something hard to find this far west. Maybe I *was* lucky.

In the few weeks since the Comanche butchered my family, I had met many kinds of people. Back on the ranch, we rarely saw a neighbor pop by more than once a month or two or even three. Once, we went for a year without seeing *anybody*. Even then, they were Pa's friends and acquaintances.

Nobody ever brought any kids to our place. I was lucky back then, though. I always had my twin brother, James. I wonder what he would think of me now and everything happening. I guess I would never know.

When the waiter came, he had pieces of paper stuck to thin wooden boards. He gave us one each.

"Raise your hand when y'all have decided what cha want," the skinny man said.

He was missing one arm and wore the remnants of a Confederate soldier. He looked like another one who abandoned what was his after the war and drifted south to Texas.

"Well, lookee there. We can pick and choose what we wanna eat. Usually, we get three of whatever they've got. Let me see. Steak, pork chops, bear, whitetail deer, and here it says rattlesnake. Or am I reading it wrong?"

"Restaurants this far west put anything they find and shoot on the menu," Malvo said. "Actually, rattlesnakes aren't bad. They sort of taste like chicken. Did ya see they have an armadillo, too? They gut it and cook it right in the shell. It tastes better than chicken."

"I'll go with the tató," Chito-Ochi said. He looked at me and said, "Armadillo—that is what my people call it."

"Here, it says the steaks weigh a pound," Malvo said. "I'll have that, but only if you let me try your tató. Order what cha want, young man. It would help if you had plenty of food to fill out and grow. In a year, you'll be as tall as me. You're almost as tall as Chito-Ochi already."

"I'll play it safe and order the venison. That and a mug of milk."

"Make that a beer." Malvo chuckled. "If you wanna drink milk, do it on your own time. We've got a reputation to keep up. A beer won't hurt anybody, but I can understand if you steer clear of the hard liquor. I believe you'll be a better man for it."

seventeen
lady's mystery

Malvo and Chito-Ochi walked into the dim room. A lamp glowed from the back, and a slight breeze from the cracked window made a candle flicker on the table. Sheriff Sam Gimbles was sitting behind his desk alone, with his head in his hands. They could hear a woman singing in the back of the cell block.

"Don't you like light, Sheriff?" Malvo asked. "How ya doing, Sam?"

"I drank too much last night, and I have a headache," the sheriff replied. "The light just makes my head throb worse."

"So, tell me about this woman I'm gonna meet," Malvo whispered as he eyed the door to the cell block. "Why is she so special she needs guarding?"

"Why do you think I got drunk last night?" Gimbles said. "I've never seen a woman talk so much. I wonder if all of them Spanish women are alike. If they are, Lord help the men. I don't know if she got a wink of sleep. She sure is full of spit and vinegar. She said she was goin' back to freshen up. That's been a spell, so she should finish any minute. She knew you were supposed to arrive today. I told her I doubt you'd make it before dark."

Malvo and Chito-Ochi pulled up seats and sat. Tanner kicked out his boots and drummed his fingers on the grips of his pistols in cross-draw holsters. If you wore your revolvers on your hips, you couldn't draw fast sitting in a chair. When he was forced to pull, every split second mattered.

The Choctaw Indian wore two pistols on a wide leather belt: one in the front and another smaller caliber in the small of his back. Large knife handles stuck out of his boots.

The sheriff pulled on his scruffy hair. He had stained his shirt with supper, and his beard was full of crumbs. A dented hat lay on the desktop.

Malvo went to comment on his filthy appearance. He believed this was no way for a city official to look, and he wasn't shy about saying so. Before he could speak, light boot heels banged against the wooden floor. An expensive European perfume wafted into the air, and all three involuntarily took a deep breath.

A woman stopped in the doorway with her fists on her hips. They could only see her silhouette with the lamplight behind her. "Buenas tardes, señores. Good afternoon, gentlemen. It took you long enough to get here. My name is Sofía García Fuentes de Alambra. I assume you are Malvo Tanner and his scout, Mr. Chito-Ochi. Did I say that correctly?"

She stepped into the room, showing her face. Her

skin was the color of light olives, and her eyes were as black as coal, but they were alive with life and what appeared to be mischief. Malvo locked eyes with the defiant woman. It was written all over her face. She wore riding boots and tight britches with leather inner legs and bottom. Despite her loose white blouse, it still showed her curves. Her raven black hair hung down her back, nearly to her waist.

"Yes, ma'am, you did," the Indian replied.

"I suppose you are wondering why I brought you here. Let me pull up a chair and tell you about my little plan and what I need for you two to do."

Two more seats hung from wooden pegs in the wall. As soon as she went to pull down a chair, the men remembered their manners, and Malvo and his friend jumped to their feet.

"Sit here, ma'am," Malvo said as he hurried to grab her chair.

"I assure you, I am very capable, Mr. Tanner," Sofía scolded. "I believe even more than most men, as a matter of fact."

"So, what do you want us to do for you?" Malvo said. "We are now officially on the clock."

"Guard my bulls," Sofía stated.

"Guard your bulls?" Malvo asked. "What exactly is that supposed to mean?"

The sheriff let a hint of a smile slip past his lips. Now, the Spanish woman was Malvo's responsibility. The sheriff was paid well, but he didn't want to have to listen to her rattle on any longer.

Sheriff Gimbles stood and said, "Since you won't be

needing me anymore, I think I'll step outside for a smoke. Maybe the cool air will clear my head." He disappeared so fast that Malvo didn't have time to protest.

"Bulls, you say?" Malvo asked. "I thought we were supposed to protect *you* from somebody."

"That, too, of course. Let me explain a little before we go any further. Men often get confused if challenged with new ideas."

Her comments flew over Chito-Ochi's head but not Malvo's. She was beginning to anger him, but he reminded himself that she was the boss, paying them handsomely.

"Go ahead," Malvo replied. "We're all ears."

"We have built a temporary bull ring down the street with waiting boxes for the bulls. Behind that is a corral where I brought two fighting bulls from Spain. I need you to protect my animals and me, as I believe some Mexicans plan to poison the bulls, and if that fails, then they will try to take my life."

"Are you sure about this, ma'am? Malvo asked. "I like getting paid good money, but I don't like to take high wages for doing nothing. Unless there is something that we still don't understand, maybe you can elaborate a little."

"It's simple. Mexican men want to kill me and my bulls, and I am paying you to stop them from succeeding. Don't worry. You will have your hands full soon enough, that I can guarantee. That was why I asked for the best. I never settle for less."

"All right then, Missus García Fuentes de Alambra. That's a mighty long name for daily use, ain't it?"

"Call me Sofía," she said, forcing a smile of full-bodied lips.

Her hair made a widow's brow peak, and her eyebrows were dark and delicate. Despite her arrogant demeanor, Malvo hadn't missed that she *was* a beauty.

"Fine, then, Sofi." Malvo smiled, but it wasn't forced like hers. He had always been attracted to Latin women.

"Don't you dare ever call me that again," the Spanish fireball spat. "That is vulgar and incorrect. My name is Sofía, not Sofi, like a dog's name. Tread carefully now, sir."

"W-w-what? All right, Sofía, I apologize for the mistake, and it won't happen again," Malvo stuttered.

The Spanish lady seemed to settle down a little and her frown disappeared. "All right, as long as we have that one thing clear, we can be on a first-name basis. That is if you don't mind, Mr. Tanner, Mr. Ochi."

The Choctaw Indian kept his mouth shut, but he couldn't help but snicker. The woman was so full of herself that he found it amusing. Especially how she twisted Malvo up; maybe he had met his match.

"Nope, Malvo is fine with me. Nobody calls me Mr. Tanner but strangers."

"So where are these bulls you're talking about? Chito-Ochi is my name. It means Handsome Water."

"What a strange name, but elegant at the same time. I doubt you like being called only Chito, either."

The Choctaw Indian looked at his best friend and

said, "Not much." This made Malvo raise both eyebrows. He was getting it from all sides today.

"When you continue down the street, you will see the new bull ring I constructed. I ordered it last year before I arrived so I would have everything ready to go. The bulls are in the back. The sheriff deputized two men standing guard with rifles, but I question their dependability. I would prefer it if you two replaced them forthwith. I will be along shortly to go into detail and explain exactly what I expect of you. It is a small arena by Spanish standards, but I only want to prove what a success it would be. Once I establish my ideas, we will begin construction of a new Feria de Torros at the edge of town. When the population grows, it will eventually be in the town center. I am sure people will come from as far as Mexico and Texas, at the very least. I am sure it will be a huge success."

Malvo and Chito-Ochi stood, turned, and headed out the door, more confused than when they walked in. They slipped their hats back on.

Fireflies flashed in one place only to light up in another. The stars seemed so close that you could reach out and grab one. Coyotes sang their perpetual choir somewhere in the dark as music floated from saloon windows and doors.

bulls & fools

Malvo, Chito-Ochi, and I walked down the street looking for the new bullfighting arena. When they told me about the meeting with the pretty Spanish lady, it sounded crazy. Who in their right minds would think grown men dancing around a corral with a red and pink cape could make money? When we reached the location, the smell of sawed pine floated in the air. We saw the wild bulls the woman talked about, and they both wore Spanish brands on their hips.

They stood in the corral, hammering the ground with a single hoof and swinging their massive heads from side to side. Their long, curved white horns looked as pointed as spears.

In the early morning, steam seeped from their large nostrils, disappearing almost instantly. The smell of wild animals was strong. I could practically feel the excitement of the town citizens, as well as the danger of the bulls.

"For the folks from Mexico, this is almost as good as

a circus," Malvo said as we walked toward the livery corral. "For some, even more. It's a tradition brought by the Spanish. Fighting bulls, like grizzlies and moose, are the only animals that don't back down. They would rather die than accept defeat."

"Gosh, they look dangerous. I wouldn't go into that corral for a thousand dollars."

"Yep, the Spanish call it the Fiesta of the Bulls, and the Mexicans adopted the name. The Conquistadores originally brought the gruesome sport to Mexico City around 1600. I once read it all started in Logroño, Spain, in 1133," Malvo said. "When I lived in Mexico City, it was the biggest sporting event, usually held on Sundays after mass. My dead wife took me, and she loved it even though I felt it was too bloody. Maybe I've already seen enough violence in my life and that was before the Civil War."

Wife? This was the first time Malvo said anything about being married. That may be why he spoke Spanish, like in Mexico. I wonder how long he stayed. Do I dare ask? Maybe when the right time comes around. I doubt now would be it. I better focus on the job at hand and ask questions over dinner.

"That is the oldest non-American Indian sport I've ever heard of," Chito said. "Our game, put the rock in the hole, is thousands of years old, long before White men came to this land."

"A Spanish fella named Hermán Cortés conquered Mexico on the thirteenth of August, 1521, so they've been around for a long time," Malvo said, holding his chin in his hand, looking over the massive black animals. "Heck, the land we stand on was Spanish. A soldier named Oñate took possession of New Mexico in 1598."

To our surprise, an apparently drunken Latin man raced toward the pen and jumped the fence with his horse. He had a red cape over his shoulder and pointed darts or pinchos in his hands. He rode with the reins in his teeth. Maybe he wasn't drunk. I could see straight away that he was an expert rider, but what in the world was he doing with those dangerous bulls?

Both torros stared at him, but one squared off and made a wild pass, nearly touching the horse as the rider speared the dart into the bull's back and delicately moved his horse to the side, skillfully dodging the sharp horns. He brazenly bowed to the small but growing crowd.

Fire burned in the eyes of the one thousand five-hundred-pound beast. I was wide-eyed as I watched the unusual spectacle. My pa had read about such bulls in books, but I didn't know the practice extended to the southern parts of the United States and all of Mexico.

Out of the corner of my eye, I saw the other bull standing in the crook of the corral when he, too, began to hammer the earth with a hoof. The rider hadn't seen the change in the other animal's eyes and was still focused on the bull he believed he was making an exhibition of.

Suddenly, the quiet beast charged the rider from his blind side, embedding its horns deep into the side of his horse's flanks. I could hear the bones crunch and the horse whooshed out a breath. The bull planted its feet, lifting it entirely off the ground. The rider had enough time to pull up his leg and avoid the horns.

His mount screamed as blood poured from the massive holes made by pointed, thick horns. The horse fell under the rider, sending him slamming to the ground. As he sat up and blinked, both bulls got him in their sights. He jumped to his feet and whipped a red cape, gracefully passing it before his body.

When the first raging bull made another pass, he gracefully sidestepped the danger, and the animal slipped under his cape. The pink underside flashed in the sunlight. He deftly slipped around the bull, avoiding his horns by no more than an inch. I held my breath, waiting to see what happened next. At that point, I was sure the Spaniard was going to die.

"In a real ring they have a burladero to hide behind so they matadors don't get killed when things get out of hand," Malvo said. "It's a square wall built of heavy timber with a bullseye painted on the front. It sits on one side of the ring, a couple of feet from the wall. It allows the matador to escape a bad situation, but the opening is too small for the bull to pass. Often, that's all that separates the matador and death. I've even seen bulls jump up and into the files of spectators, making them scatter. Sometimes, it gets dangerous for the viewers, too."

"What is a matador?"

"Matador means killer, but then again, sometimes the bulls kill the man. When this happens, the wild animal wins. At least they give him a fighting chance. Most bullfighters bear the scars of their opponents' horns, and many die young. Still, it's a great honor to be such a person in Mexico. Now it appears Miss Sofía wants it to happen here in New Mexico. She claims there are fortunes to make, just like south of here. We probably have enough Mexicans around here to make up a crowd."

"But why do we have to protect her *and* her bulls? I don't understand—it just doesn't make sense to me. Sure, a woman can always use someone to look out for her west of Texas, but to guard a couple of bulls? Maybe this Sofi woman is as crazy as Maude Granger."

"Make sure you don't call her Sofi to her face—or crazy, for that matter," Chito-Ochi said. "Malvo did, and she gave him an earful. She is a brash woman if I ever saw one."

We didn't hear her come up behind us. It was anybody's guess how long she had been standing there listening and watching. I suddenly wondered if she heard me call her Sofi, and I turned as red as a beet.

"To prepare the bulls for a fight, we hold them in a small room with no light and no water or food," Sofía said as though she hadn't been eavesdropping. "This leaves the bull confused and anxious, so when he comes out and into the grand ring, he is furious and ready to fight."

"Your man there just about got himself killed," Malvo said. "His horse is already dead, and if you don't get him out of there, he might be next."

"He was foolish to go in there without the horse's armor, but don't worry about him. He is a professional torero from Salamanca, Spain. That is where they breed and raise the best bulls. Aggression has been in their blood for decades."

"May I ask a question, ma'am?"

She looked at me like she hadn't noticed me before then. Standing beside men like Malvo and Chito-Ochi, I didn't look like much. I could feel my face turn red again.

"And who are you, young man?" Sofía said with a thick European accent. "How old are you? I'd guess you're seventeen or so."

I stood tall when she said she thought I was two years older than I was. I wonder if Miranda felt the same. I never told her my age.

"I'm Benji Willow, and I ride with Malvo and Chito-Ochi. I reckon I'm working for you now, ma'am."

She looked surprised, even though she did a good job hiding it. I preferred her thinking I was seventeen. I liked that much better. She was not a bad-looking woman for her age. She must be all of forty. For me, that's usually very old, but some special gracefulness about her made her seem younger. I noticed Malvo's face. When she wasn't looking, he eyed her up and down as Chito-Ochi watched his friend—little curls formed on the edge of his lips.

"So, what is your question, Benji Willow?" She smiled, humoring me.

She could tell I had a little crush on her already. Malvo might have one, too. Then again, a woman like her probably had a lot of men interested. I liked her, and I was only in my teens.

"I understand standing guard over an educated woman like yourself, but why in the world would you want us to guard livestock if they are locked up in pens?"

"I propose to introduce bullfighting to America, and there are certain Mexican breeders and politicians that don't like what I'm doing. If they had the chance, they may poison my bulls. Fighting bulls are very expensive, and Mexican breeders make a living raising and selling them. Remember, most bulls die after their first bullfight. Only special bulls win the honor to remain alive, so there is always a market for fresh animals. But they can't be just any bull. We breed ours to be particularly mean. Some bulls are worth more than a house here in town. There is a small fortune exchanging hands in the bullfighting world, not to mention the exuberant wages the matadors get. They make more money than the baseball players of the New York Nine or the Knickerbockers."

"Gosh, who would have ever imagined an old bull could be worth so much money."

"These are not just any bulls," Sofía replied. "I plan to bring animals from Salamanca, where these two were bred. I will develop my own breeding farm if my plan is successful. Those two beautiful black animals' lives are paramount to my plan. The Mexican against my idea might even go as far as trying to kill me, too. You cannot imagine how much money is involved in bull-fighting in places like Mexico City and Leon, Guanajuato. If I breed better bulls than them, they will go out of business. I even brought my own matador to complete the presentation. There are few Mexican matadors that rank with Spain's best. We already have fliers across Mexico, Texas, Arizona, and New Mexico, offering a prize to the local matador up to the challenge."

In the corral, a half dozen men had already herded the bulls into their pens with hurdles and whips. Others used a mule to drag off the dead horse. The matador walked our way, and Sofía's face lit up.

"This is Alejandro del Torres." Sofía smiled. "He is a professional matador from Madrid and one of Spain's best."

I doffed my hat as the men shook hands. Despite my gun, they seemed to see me as a boy. I was going to have to do something about that.

Feeling left out, I wandered from the corral while my new friends discussed what they should be looking for and what could go wrong. I decided to go for a ride and headed for the stables and my horse. I needed some time to think. I believed I was up to much more than Malvo and Chito-Ochi thought, but I didn't know how to relay the fact.

A man rushed up beside me, and as soon as I mounted, he grabbed my bridle and wrenched the reins from my hands. The man was the same obnoxious lieutenant from back on the trail to Socorro. He was angry about how Malvo embarrassed him, and he planned to take his revenge on me.

"Let go of my horse before I shoot ya, fool!"

I wrapped my fingers around my pistol's grip and put my thumb on the hammer, but the angry soldier didn't back down. He growled and jerked the bit so hard my horse squealed. My face flushed red, and my anger soured like never before. Just as I was about to pull my Colt Walker, a horse bumped into mine, jolting me.

Suddenly, Malvo appeared at my side. He shucked a boot backward out of his stirrup and kicked the man, trying to grab my horse. It was Lieutenant Bentley, and he wanted to get even for what Tanner had done to him in the desert. I remembered his puggy face. After he had a boot stuck in his, he looked different.

The officer moved his tongue around and spat out three teeth. He growled, showing a bloody mouth, but he backed down. His shirt-stained red as claret flowed freely from his busted lips. In a minute, they swelled to twice their normal size.

Malvo turned to me. I could see the concern on his face. He looked at me like my pa used to when I was a kid. It made me feel good that he cared, but still, I wanted to prove I was a man. I appreciated him helping me, but it was time I stood up for myself. I didn't want my partners to have to pull my weight. I could do it on my own.

"I was just about to shoot him. I warned him, too, but he wouldn't back away. He grabbed my horse and said he was gonna take it from me. Horse thieves get shot in Texas."

"If we were back in El Paso and Sheriff Cassidy was on the job, you just might have gotten away with it. Shooting military men is another thing, though. Don't you know the army would track you down if you shot him, right or wrong? Had you killed him, you would have found yourself before a judge and an angry jury. Quite a few reckless young men are running around New Mexico, ready to use their guns, and they've already strung up more than one. Sometimes even tarred and feathered. When you're in a town without connections with the law, you've gotta tread lightly."

"Yeah, I guess you're right. I've never been that angry before, though. I know I was ready to shoot him before I'd let him take my horse. I know from the ranch it's a hanging offense—my pa told me so. If things were fair, he should be the one that needs to be careful."

"Next time, if you must, take the safe and legal way, even though it sounds worse. Let him take the horse, and when he mounts up and rides away, shoot him in the back as he escapes. Then you're within the boundaries of the law, and he'd be considered a horse thief. If you shoot him just like that without him threatening your life, you could end up on the wrong end of a rope. The law is funny like that."

"But you're friends with Sheriff Gimbles, aren't you? He would back us up as honest men, wouldn't he?"

"He wouldn't know an honest man if he smacked him in the face. I doubt there are a dozen men in all Socorro who trust the sheriff any further than they can throw him. He's lowlife trash with a badge. Just because a man claims to be a lawman doesn't mean that it's true. Oh, sure, he wears a star, but there are many ways to acquire tin."

I blinked like a chick in a nest as I listened in awe.

"Never take the law for face value. Look at Boon, all dressed up in fancy duds, smiling all the time. The truth is he's killed more men than anybody I know, and most of them were when he wasn't wearin' a badge. Who knows what the circumstances were? There are a dozen variations to what happens in every gunfight. Like I say, just because they wear tin that says sheriff or marshal don't mean that they're honest."

I guessed I would have to look at everything differently. The law sounded much more complicated than I thought. I always believed it cut and dry—black and white. Now, there seemed to be shades of gray in place of my old image of lawmen.

"Who should I trust, then, Malvo?"

"Your friends and nobody else until they prove themselves worthy. Even then, keep an eye out because people change like the direction of the wind."

nineteen
the grand event

Despite Sofía's paranoia, nothing had happened so far. It was the day before the big event, and the bulls were fine. As far as we could tell, nobody had come around to bother the Spanish woman. Everything had been so quiet it was almost eerie. We spent days waiting for nothing. We were so bored that we resorted to tossing cards into an upturned hat and playing one-deck faro.

We were in the middle of town, so I had to abandon my target practice for now. I didn't like that because I had been practicing every day, and I was just beginning to get better fast. I cleaned my guns daily for something to do.

I watched the curious, massive black bulls from all the way across the ocean—places that I couldn't even imagine. Why in the world would someone breed bulls to be any meaner than the Texan ones already were?

By dark, people were spreading out bedrolls in the street and getting ready to sleep on and under porches. We moved into a home Missus Sofía rented right next door to hers. It had plenty of room, and our own outhouse was out back.

But we spent most of our time sitting on the porch so we could keep the bulls in plain sight. At night, we took turns standing watch on the outside of the corral with Winchesters in the crooks of our arms. Our presence was enough to ward off the problems the Spanish lady foresaw.

That was until the people began to arrive. Most of the visitors were Mexican, but there were White folks, what the Spanish called Gringos, from all around New Mexico, Texas, and Arizona, too. That morning, they started to dribble in a dozen or two at a time.

At first, we thought the grand event would be a bust and only some would attend. All that hard work and money Sofía spent would have all been for nothing.

By noon, they arrived in their twenties and thirties, and one group was at least fifty strong. Eventually, we had to move to the corral because there were so many people around that we couldn't see across the street. That night, hundreds of visitors descended on Socorro and slept in every square inch of land not covered by a building. A few even resorted to climbing up to the back of houses and sleeping on roofs.

When a rooster crowed on the chair next to mine, I lost my balance and fell on my butt. I had been sleeping in it, leaning against the building, with my feet dangling in the air. It brought snickers from Malvo and Chito-Ochi, much to my dismay. I had been doing well, but I couldn't stay awake.

Sunlight crept from the horizon westward and across the town. In minutes, people began to murmur and stir as hundreds awoke. In no time, whispers become a roaring crowd. There were only a few hours until the grand event.

"Let me go get Sofía before she takes a mind to cross this mess of humanity by herself," Malvo said as he eyed the street, looking for a clear path to the other side.

When noon struck in the church bell tower, the small bullfighting arena was bursting at the seams, and hundreds stood outside trying to hear what was happening. They had all gotten a peek of the bulls the night before when they were put on show.

I thought I saw a few suspicious-looking characters then, but when I looked again, I wasn't so sure. Most of the Mexicans looked pretty much alike because I wasn't accustomed to seeing so many foreigners at once. My mind was flooded with faces while I tried to determine who was dangerous and who wasn't.

The bullfight began when the mysterious Latin lady dropped a white hanky into the ring. This officially commenced the game. The provisional bullring was sizable, but Malvo said it was smaller than those in Mexico City. He said they held thousands of people. It had become a tradition, just like on the Iberian Peninsula in Southern Europe.

When the gate opened, and the thousand-five-hundred-pound bull stormed out and ran wild-eyed around the ring, the crowd went nuts. I began to feel the contagiousness of the mass of people watching their favorite sport of some seven hundred years. Before I knew it, I, too, was cheering and clapping—at least until Chito-Ochi gave me a stern look.

"You can't watch for trouble and get drawn into the crowd at the same time," the Choctaw Indian warned. "Watch but keep your eyes in the back of your head open."

I know I didn't have eyes in the back of my head, but I got what he was on about. Every little bit, I had a good look around and at the crowd. We were standing behind a barrier called a *burladero,* which gave the bullfighters access to safety when they needed to escape the ring and the bull's horns.

The men were dressed in the fanciest short britches and shirts I've ever seen. But I didn't like the hats at all. They provided no shade for a man living in Texas and sat on their heads sideways.

"Those are the picadors," Malvo said. "See those darts they have in their hands? They ride horses right up to a dangerous bull and stab it in the back with three or four darts to make it angrier. They are some of the best riders I've ever seen. Look how gracefully they dodge the bull."

When I saw the bull run by me after the picadors stuck the darts in its back, red blood contrasted with the black coat of hair. I suddenly felt sorry for the animal. They were torturing it to make it meaner for when it would finally face the matador, and I knew what matador meant. It was Spanish for killer. I had seen Alejandro brandishing a long sword.

Maybe the bull would win and kill the matador. Would that be fair justice?

"Why in the world would they wanna do something like that? I don't think I like where this is going."

Roars raced through the crowd when the picadors rode across the ring with long, pointed darts in their hands. Their horses wore thick leather armor to fend off the bull's dangerous horns.

I could hear a horn trumpet from somewhere behind the mass of humanity. It was the signal for the matador to challenge the bull. As the wild black beast ran in circles, Alejandro walked calmly into the middle of the ring as if the beast weren't even there. He had his fancy red cape over his shoulder, and he held his strange black hat high in his hand, offering his display to the crowd.

I realized Sofía was right when I saw the second bull burst out of the box, jump out of the ring and storm into the crowd. People began to scream and scatter. Alejandro turned to see what was happening. That was when his bull hooked his horns into his backside and tossed him high into the air. His sword lay broken on the ground.

"It's happening!" Malvo shouted. "Somebody let the other bull out!"

Suddenly, I was running behind Chito-Ochi and Malvo as we raced around the inside of the ring to the far side. Malvo grabbed the Spanish woman and tossed her over his shoulder as we continued to run.

I could see nearly a ton of black hair charge through the spectators, tossing people into the air left and right.

Others were trampled under the bull's hooves as it snorted and pawed the ground, swinging its head from side to side.

The gunshot was loud and made my ears ring. I looked to my side, and smoke rolled out of Chito-Ochi's Henry rifle barrel. He fired two more rounds into the bull's brain. It resisted for a moment until it dropped to its knees, blood pouring from its mouth.

Sofía screamed, "No! Don't kill my precious bulls!"

"We've no choice, ma'am," Chito-Ochi replied. "It was killing people." He looked into the bullring at the other dangerous animal, frowning.

"Alejandro," Sofía whispered as the scene took her breath away.

Her matador lay on the ground, bleeding out. When the bull gored his bottom, it ripped out his guts. Alejandro stared sightlessly at the sky. Chito-Ochi raised his rifle a second time and killed the second bull. They were too dangerous to allow to live.

The local politicians would have had them put down anyway. Now, they must try to keep the Spanish woman out of jail. She was responsible for all this mess.

"Get the Española!" the locals cried. "She did this!"

Some sat kneeling beside the wounded and broken loved ones while their eyes looked for the Spanish woman. In minutes, Sheriff Gimbles was racing our way with pistols in his fists.

"All right, everybody, get on out of here, now! The doctor and nurse are on their way. What a foolish idea, ma'am. I'm afraid you're gonna have come with me. I've got to lock you up for your own safety. I'm afraid you had better get yourself a good lawyer, too. You've been the cause of many injured people here today. Some may even die."

"Gosh." I stood beside Malvo, frowning, but there was nothing we could do. "What are we gonna do now? We probably won't even get paid."

"We don't do anything," Malvo replied. "Our job here is done. We might have had to sacrifice the bulls, but we saved Sofía's life. Hadn't we been there, the Mexicans that let that bull out would have got ahold of her. They'd have tarred and feathered her before they strung her up. Now, I reckon she'll get jailed until her connections back home get her out. Don't worry, they will. I don't think bullfighting is such a good idea for New Mexico. I doubt it would work in Texas, either."

"It was her fault this happened," Chito-Ochi said. "It was a fool's notion if you ask me, but still, it was good money for us."

"But now that she's in jail, we'll never get paid, and we were the ones that saved the day from that crazy woman."

"Do we look like foolish men?" Malvo asked.

"No, sir. I *know* you're not foolish men."

"That's why we always get paid in advance." Malvo shrugged. "You know that first day when we sent you to the dinner to save us seats? We were paid then and there. I thought you knew, especially as the woman was a foreigner. That's what that good, honest reputation of ours brings. She came to us, and we never work without getting paid in advance. God knows, this far west, anything could happen at any time."

I was still upset from seeing all the damage the crazy bulls had done, but I was relieved I would get paid for these sixteen days' work. I needed a change of clothing badly. I was tired of wearing the rags of a poor boy.

The only thing I owned that was in decent shape were my chaps, which I only wore when I traveled in the country. There was little use for them in town.

return to el paso

"What do you think is going to happen to that Spanish woman? I can't see such an elegant lady in jail. I saw what Sheriff Gimbles' cells looked like. They were for hardened criminals."

After the first day's ride back to Texas and El Paso, we sat around the campfire. We weren't in a hurry on the return trip, so we planned to take four days to do what we did ten days ago in less than three. Malvo said he didn't have to be back for a week, so nobody was in a hurry. The Choctaw Indian seemed to follow along wherever he went.

An owl hooted in the night, and a minute later, its mate cooed back. Crickets chirped off and on with their nightly chatter. The perpetual coyotes howled in the distance, yelping at the moon as it glowed over the horizon. The smell of burning wood filled the air, and the fire kept the desert night chill at bay.

"If you were the cause of the problem and the law gets broken, you too would go to jail," Malvo said, "even if it wasn't your intention. It's called manslaughter in the first degree."

"Manslaughter? Is that worse than murder? In the first degree? That sounds mighty bad. Do you think they'll hang Miss Sofía?"

"It may sound it, but it ain't as bad a murder," Malvo replied. "Especially if it's not premeditated. It's an unintentional death dealt out by a perpetrator. It's just like if you ran over a woman while recklessly racing your wagon through town. No matter how you look at it, you'd have still killed someone, and the law would make you responsible. In the end, you would go before a jury. Then, they would decide your fate, which could go pretty much any way. You never know what twelve jurors might decide. It's all up to the toss of a coin unless you have money and a corrupt lawyer with connections. Whichever way it goes, it's no longer our business. That's why we're heading home."

"I don't believe the town will be very forgiving of Sofía," Chito-Ochi said. "She was too arrogant and talked down to everybody. Now, they will remember how she was, and it may set her conviction in stone. There are going to be some angry people back in Socorro. Especially if a person from a rich family was injured or died, then she might even hang, although it's rare to see a woman executed, even in New Mexico where there is not much law."

"What about the people responsible for letting the bull out of the pen when it charged into the crowd?"

"They were probably long gone and over the border

in an hour," Chito-Ochi said. "It's only nine miles to Mexico."

"Plus, we weren't paid to chase down villains. Sure, we got paid to protect the bulls, but ultimately, it was the woman's life that was the most important," Malvo said. "Once the *torros* were a menace, they had to go. She was more important than a couple of animals, and once one was out and in the crowd, all that went up in smoke. Still, I reckon we did what we were paid for, even if I don't much like bullfighting."

"I didn't like it at all. It looked like it was a slow torture for the bulls. I hunt and all, but I always like to make a clean shot, so the animal doesn't suffer. That sport was all about the bull suffering and then getting slayed. They were noble-looking animals, too, weren't they? Why couldn't folks just leave them alone?"

"That matador paid the ultimate price," Chito-Ochi huffed. "That one killed him fast. I believe he let his attention waver at the wrong time."

"Only a crazy person would step into a closed ring with a normal bull, let alone one of them a Spanish fighting bull. I've been chased by too many to trust them."

"It takes all kinds," Malvo said. "In some places, bullfighting is as common as checkers."

I sat and stared into the fire that night for the longest time, well after Chito-Ochi and Malvo turned in. I thought about the Spanish lady sitting back in a dark jail cell. I had a hard time imagining it. She was the last person I expected to end up behind bars.

We rode on for three eventless days. All we saw were

buzzards and heat. At midday, it was almost unbear-able. I was surprised how much the weather changed from that on the Red River. It was so hot at times it felt hard to breathe, yet Malvo and Chito-Ochi seemed to thrive on it. I guess I'll eventually get used to it, just like them.

We rode into El Paso four and a half days after we left Socorro. When we walked our horses into town and wheeled toward the stables, things seemed much calmer than back in New Mexico. There wasn't much law here, either, but there was a bit more than there. At least we didn't see any Indians. For the money, things hadn't been dangerous at all.

new duds

When I walked into the store, I knew exactly what I wanted. I had been there enough times, window-shopping. I believed if I were sharp-dressed, I would look older. Of course, I didn't want a string tie and a white shirt like Boon. Then again, he considered himself a lady's man, and I knew I wasn't.

I only wanted to look good for Miranda and presentable to her father. But if I could, I would also try to look a year or two older. I was tired of people acting like I wasn't there, due to my age. They always saw and talked to me as an afterthought. I was dying to become a man.

"Howdy, mister. I was looking for a new set of duds —boots, hat, and all."

"Well, now, young man, that sounds fine and dandy, but you have to have money to buy fancy clothing," the tailor and bootmaker said as he inspected my tattered clothing, frowning.

When I pulled out five double eagles, his mouth

shut like a trap, and his eyes got greedy. He suddenly smiled from one ear to the other. I thought his face was going to break. I finally had his undivided attention.

"I work for a living, mister. I ride with Malvo Tanner and the Choctaw scout. We just came back from New Mexico, where we were protecting an important woman."

"Well, well, why didn't you say so in the first place? Where should we start? First, that hat and those old broken-down boots must go, and I just got a brand-new white Stetson in stock. It arrived only yesterday. You better get it while you can because, despite the high price, it will only last for a day or two."

I blinked, wondering how much it would be. But as soon as he turned around with it in his hands, I knew I wanted it. I'd never seen a hat I liked more in my life. It was far better, hands down, than any hat in the store.

"How much would this one set me back, sir?"

"I don't even know if I should offer it to you, youngster. Well, try it on anyway. Let's see if it fits. It won't matter what it costs if it's too big or small. A hat must fit perfectly to be comfortable. A good hat is also a useful tool against the sun, and especially white. It reflects the rays instead of absorbing them like a black hat. Here in South Texas, your headgear is almost as important as your horse and gun."

As soon as he said it, I knew it wouldn't fit. It would be too much to ask for. Heck, I had yet to inquire how much it was, anyway. For all I knew, it was a small fortune. Then again, I just got my first wages, and it was a hundred dollars less expenses. For the first time in my life, I may have changed the Willow family's luck. Maybe we wouldn't be poor people forever like we had been for as long as any of my family could remember.

I felt good about the money I had in my pocket. Maybe from now on I would prosper and grow. One day, maybe I would have a reputation like Malvo Tanner and possibly even a home and wife like he had at one time long ago.

The store clerk delicately held the brim in two hands as he hovered it over my head. It was a hand tall at the crown and had a wide but stiff brim. As soon as he dropped it on, we saw it fit as snugly as a bug. The new hat made me look like a different man.

"Why, you look like a young man instead of a teenager. I've never seen a hat change a fella so much. It certainly does the trick."

I don't know if he was being a good salesman or was being honest. I preferred to believe the latter. Now, I knew, no matter the price, the Stetson was going home with me, even if I had to return barefoot.

"So, how much does it cost, mister?"

"One double eagle," the tailor said.

"Gosh, twenty dollars? I thought you were gonna say a hundred. I'll take it. Now, let's have a look at your boots. I like black."

"You might wanna take your off chaps first, young man. I reckon you'll want a new shirt and britches too, won't you? Maybe a new belt? From the looks of things, a new pair of long johns, too. Do ya like red? White gets dirty too easily. As you're friends with

Malvo, I'll give you a special price. Come along, and I'll help ya pull off them old things you got on your feet. We'll replace them with some calf-high riding boots. How will that suit ya, sir?"

When he said 'sir,' I nearly dropped to the floor. It was the first time in my life anybody called me that. It was usually boy or son. He made my head spin a little, but I felt myself stand taller and puffed out my chest. I sure did feel like a new *man*.

"Can I have a look in the mirror, mister?"

"Let's get you dressed first, then you can have a look and see if you like the change or not."

When I walked out of the store, I was forty dollars lighter, but I looked so different when I saw my reflection in the mirror; I hardly recognized myself. I had to look over my shoulder to make sure it wasn't somebody behind me I was seeing. I patted my chest with the palms of my hands, happy, and grinned like a Cheshire Cat.

Just wait until Miranda Frank sees me. I'm going to knock her off her feet. I can see us walking down the street now.

duty calls

I had all these plans to dress up in my new duds and visit Miranda at the Frank hardware store. I hoped if her pa saw me dressed like a man, he would think I was older and worthy of his daughter's time. When I was just about to step through the door, Malvo came running up to say one of the town banks had been robbed, and Wells Fargo wanted us to track down the men and bring back the outlaws and the money.

"Why don't they send the sheriff? It's his job to catch bandits if they rob the town bank. Running down bank robbers sounds like dangerous business."

"Not if they've run for Juarez like we think," Malvo replied. "Wells Fargo don't care where they went. They just want the money returned. An American lawman can't just ride into Mexico and bring a man back because they're out of their jurisdiction. The sheriff's badge doesn't mean anything there, and Boon has too much on his hands here to run off and chase them across the country. They offered us ten percent of the loot if we recovered what they stole. That could be a considerable amount of money."

"How much did they take?"

"The bank said it was substantial but didn't want to go into detail." Malvo huffed. "I guess they don't want every Tom, Dick, and Harry out lookin' for the loot. That ain't exactly how I like it, but they've never cheated us before. They've been a customer a few times over the years and have treated us fair and square. I guess we'll have to trust *them* this time."

"I thought you always charged in advance. Now you're not only breaking your rules, but you don't even know how much money they're going to pay?"

"That is true," Chito-Ochi replied. "But you will find that as you grow up, sometimes the rules are made to be broken. We think this is one of those times."

I didn't know what that was supposed to mean, but I wasn't in the habit of questioning my elders. I guess as I'm the man on the bottom of the totem pole, I'd go along and do as I was told. Chasing down bank robbers put me into unknown waters. The first job was easy, even if it did turn into a mess, not that wasn't any fault of ours.

Maybe Malvo was right. It could turn into a substantial amount of money—possibly even more than a hundred dollars each. Maybe a thousand? I shook my head at such wild ideas, then instantly told myself not to be stupid. I'd probably never see a thousand dollars at once in my lifetime, and I knew nobody in my family had.

I would be more than happy if I could make

another hundred dollars or even fifty. As a cowboy, it would take me a month to make that much money working seven days a week. Then again, I wouldn't be risking my life like we would be once we crossed the border on the Rio Grande. I guess I signed on for better or for worse, though. I would be too ashamed to back out now, especially since I'd already seen a good payday. What would Miranda think if I up and quit? I don't want to go back to working as a drover or be lonely somewhere riding the line.

We did protect the Spanish lady, even though she ended up in jail. But chasing down men who had guns and were willing to use them was something that I hadn't come up against before. I suddenly wondered how I would react to being shot at. Sure, I knew how to use my gun and was getting handy, too. But I had a feeling it was an entirely different thing when someone was shooting back.

I hadn't given it too much thought, although I already knew what Malvo and Chito-Ochi did for a living. Still, I signed on with Tanner, knowing that all sorts of jobs could come our way. I had better stay on my toes if I didn't want to catch a bullet. I didn't survive the Comanche attack just to get winged by some lowlife outlaw. I wouldn't want to see Miranda with bullet holes in my new shirt or hat.

It was already late, so we spent the two hours before sunset checking out traveling kits and cleaning our weapons. We also went to the town armory and stocked up on .38, .44, and .45 cartridges. We didn't have time to load empty casings ourselves because we would ride out the next day before daylight. We came back from the store with piles of boxes. It looked like we were getting ready for a war.

It looked like Malvo was expecting trouble because we were much heavier armed than before. We expected to be in Mexico when the sun rose. It wouldn't do us any good to go before because the Choctaw scout had to locate the robbers' tracks first, and he couldn't do it in the dark.

Chito-Ochi would be in charge from then on. He would have to find their trail unless we found out the outlaws stopped in Juarez, but Malvo didn't think they would make it that easy. The bankers told him they seemed to know what they were doing, so this wouldn't be their first dance.

The following day, we were sitting in the diner at five sharp. That was when they opened for breakfast. I was nervous, and it just made me even hungrier than normal. Usually, I could eat everybody out of house and home. I smelled fresh bacon frying as the odor drifted through the air. My mouth began to water, and my stomach grumbled. I pulled a piece of bread off a loaf in the middle of the table and gobbled it down.

"Three full breakfasts and an extra stack of flapjacks for the sharp-dressed young man." Malvo smiled when the waiter approached. He sipped a cup of steaming hot coffee. "Maybe you better bring another loaf of bread, too. This one will probably disappear before the food comes. While you're at it, put a double portion of bacon on mine."

"I'll take double bacon, too—if that's all right." I

could hear my belly grumble some more just at the thought. I sipped the coffee before testing it and burned my mouth, but that didn't slow me down when he sat a plate of food on the table right under my nose. "Pass the honey, please." I had the knife and fork ready in my hands. I smacked my lips, and my mouth salivated.

"Be careful he doesn't bite your fingers." Chito-Ochi chuckled. "I've never seen anybody so hungry— all the time."

I could hear the door open and close, but I was too busy eating to peek. Boot heels hammered the floor, and Malvo looked up and saw the badge. He asked, "What are you doing up so early, Sheriff? You usually don't rise with the chickens like us."

Boon Cassidy slid into a seat next to me and signaled to bring another breakfast and coffee for him, too. For some reason, when he was around, he made me nervous. He never did anything bad to me, though. It was just an edgy feeling I had, and I didn't know why.

Still, I knew I should be polite to my elders, even if I secretly distrusted them or suspected they were danger-ous. Maybe it was because of the odd comment Malvo and Chito-Ochi made. I could be wrong. It probably took a hard man to tame such a lawless town as El Paso, and it looked like he was doing a pretty good job. He certainly was the politest of the bunch and always dressed sharp and dapper.

"How much are they paying you?" Boon asked in a near whisper as his eyes shot around suspiciously.

"I doubt they'd appreciate my giving out confidential information, Boon. You know how the banks are."

"It's me, Malvo. You know I ain't gonna tell anybody. I wanna know what I missed out on. The fools would have to ride south and not north. Then I would have been after them myself."

"Even still, Sheriff." Malvo huffed. "If it gets out I wagged my jaw, it may end my business with the bank. They hire me for one thing or another several times a year. Sometimes, it's just to guard a shipment or a large payroll, but still, they always pay good money. They can't get personalized service like that from you, Sheriff. You're far too busy with El Paso crime. Then again, it was much worse before you arrived. It was pretty much pure chaos."

"So, are ya gonna tell me or not?" Boon asked, frowning.

Malvo knew he had to tell him. He was the town law, after all. "If I hear this from anyone else, I'll know it's you because we ain't talked to nobody about nothin'."

I saw Chito-Ochi's eyes, and they told Malvo not to talk, but he didn't notice, and I didn't have the nerve to point it out.

"Ten percent of the haul," Malvo whispered, eyeing anyone nearby. "Whatever that is. They didn't come right out and tell us how much they stole."

"Whew," Boon said. "I thought it was going to be a lot of money. You know the bank doesn't keep that much cash around except on Fridays and Saturdays when the payrolls are paid in town. Now I'm glad I didn't have to go. You might be looking at a whole lot of riding for very little money, pard."

Cassidy snickered and blew on his coffee. He seemed as pleased as punch. I couldn't say the same for Malvo. He looked like he would be grumpy for the next few hours. For me, anything was better than no money at all. The way I saw it, it was all a bonus, and I couldn't go wrong as long as I didn't get shot.

I had to put my faith in Malvo and Chito-Ochi. They'd been doing this for a long time, and I didn't see them missing any digits or limbs. They were still upright and breathing. I tried to push the danger out of my mind. Then the food came, and I forgot everything but my stomach.

Nobody said a word for ten minutes as we devoured fried eggs, sausages, baked beans, and bacon in quantity. Knives and forks scraped tin pie pans clean. There was even the occasional belch. Soon, all the food was gone.

I didn't look up until I grabbed the last bit of bread to wipe the yolk from my pan. When I did have a peek, everybody looked at me as if I came from another planet. I guess they'd never seen me eat when I was nervous.

"You must have a hollow leg," Boon said in wonder. "I have no idea where all that food goes. You would think you'd be as fat as a whale."

twenty-three
out of commission

After breakfast, we lit out like we were being chased by a hundred Comanche. It was only minutes until the first crack of dawn, so we stretched into a gallop to make the river, which was on the edge of town. We raced across El Paso and down to the best place to ford El Rio Grande. We got there as the first traces of light began to sparkle on the water's surface.

Chito-Ochi dropped off his horse and kneeled by the river's edge. "They didn't waste time covering their tracks where they crossed. It looks like they planned to run hard and long. They must know that somebody is going to come after them. I hope they haven't gained too much on us."

"They couldn't have," Malvo said, "unless they traveled all night. Then again, that's what I would have done. Maybe put as much distance from any law that might follow and the outlaws as possible. Let's go," Malvo added, gigging his horse as it splashed into the water.

The river was up from the recent rain, and it soon covered the horses' bellies, and got our boots wet, but we continued to push through the river fast. As we pushed across the surface waters, wakes followed. The early morning sun reflected off the surface making us squint our eyes, but still I was partially blinded.

A loud gunshot rang out completely surprising me. We hadn't even been looking. We were so focused on getting after the bank robbers, we got a little lax. I ducked my head but felt the air crack as the bullet whizzed by.

"Come on, move it!" Malvo yelled as he spurred his horse to the other side with a pistol in his hand.

Three more shots were fired kicking up water beside us. The gunfire was getting closer with every blast. We reached the south side of the river and gigged our horses up the banks. Their eyes were spread wide in fright just like mine. When I was almost to the top, my spare horse slipped and fell, pulling me off my mount. A man walked his horse out of the building's shadows as he raised his rifle one last time and took aim. The gun was pointing right at me. I went for my Colt Walker, but I knew I was too late. He already had me in my sights.

The blur of a horse entered my side vision as Malvo screamed then he flashed before my eyes racing past me. Before the outlaw could react, Tanner's horse crashed into his, knocking him to the ground. Both men were sent flying through the air. The outlaw crashed through the front window of a home, breaking the glass. His body lay over the windowsill and he suddenly went still.

A piece of glass as large as a mirror protruded from his back. It had sliced right through his heart and he was killed instantly.

When I looked around, I saw Malvo lying on the ground, and he wasn't moving, either. My heart jumped into my mouth as it tried to beat its way out of my chest.

"Chito-Ochi! Malvo is down!"

Sweat rolled down my face. It hadn't been lost on my how close I came to getting shot and maybe even killed. I wheeled my horse and sprinted up the bank to Malvo's side. When I dropped to the ground, I kneeled beside him. I laid his head in my lap as tears streaked the dust on my face. I neared my ear to his mouth and I could just make out his breath.

"He's still breathin'!" I felt his neck for a pulse, and it was there although it seemed to be weak and erratic. Malvo's face was the color of death. "Come on, Chito-Ochi. He's down but I can't see where he's shot." Blood made a small dark pool under his head.

"It looks like he hit his head when the horses clashed and fell." The Indian glanced at the outlaw. "That one is dead, and it looks like he was alone. They probably had him hang back to bushwhack us as we forded the river."

"What are we gonna do? We can't let him die."

Chito-Ochi grabbed Malvo and slung him over his shoulder then lay him across his spare horse's back.

"We must get him to a doctor before he dies."

I blinked, confused. Malvo had always seemed indestructible and now he was limp as a rag, and he had a gash in the back of his head leaving his thick hair sticky with blood.

"We've got to get him help," Chito-Ochi said. "There is a clinic three blocks down."

When he had him lying over the horse's back, the Indian pushed up his eyelids with his thumb, but Malvo's eyes had already crawled back into his skull. Then Chito-Ochi shook his head, his mouth no more than a gash. His brow was wrinkled like an old goatskin.

When we reached a white plaque that said, *Pedro Paloma, Doctor General y Dentista*, I ran up and banged on the door. I knew it was early, but I wasn't about to wait. Malvo could be teetering between life and death. He was still breathing but all the color had drained from his face.

Grumbling came from inside. Somebody said, "Espera, que voy! I'm coming, just you wait."

When the door opened, a small man dressed more like an undertaker than a doctor or dentist stood and blinked as he rubbed his hands.

"What do you want, young man?" His dark face crinkled into a knowing smile. "Did ya get a dose from the brothels? Cowboys come and visit here all the time. That's why I speak such good English."

"No, sir, I don't frequent such places." I pointed back to Malvo over a horse's back. "It's my friend. He fell and hit his head. He's been out ever since."

The doctor frowned. "Bring him in, quick. Lay him on the table there on the side of the room so I can examine him."

Chito-Ochi got his shoulders, and I got his feet, and we struggled to get the large man up and onto the operating table. When we lay him down, more blood pooled under his head. It slowly seeped from a gash in his skull.

"How did this happen? I'm Dr. Paloma." He pointed to the sign. It was in small letters at the bottom. "All right then, go on over there and sit down and stay out of my way. Let me give your friend a good examination and I can tell you what I think."

"Is he going to live?" I could hardly keep my teeth from chattering.

The doctor gave me a stern look and eyed the chairs. I did as I was told and sat but I moved around like I had ants in my pants. I was as nervous as a rat in a box trap.

Chito-Ochi sat to wait, his face a mask. Just from looking at him, I knew it would do no good to talk. When he went like that, he closed up like a clam. He patiently waited as the doctor looked our friend over. Finally, the doctor shook his head, clucking his tongue and turned toward us in the corner. We sat as still as statues waiting to hear the verdict.

"Is he relation to you two? Is he your pa, boy?" the doctor asked.

I shook my head as my eyes watered up. I had to fight back the tears or embarrass myself.

"No, sir, we ride together," Chito-Ochi replied. "We aren't related but we are like family. What do you think? Will he wake up?"

"Oh, I reckon he could wake up all right," the

doctor replied. "Time will tell if there was any damage suffered in the fall. It looks like he had a pretty hard bang against something. It's hard to say with injuries like this."

"He hit his head on the ground when his horse fell. He was trying to save me from an outlaw with a gun."

"You don't say. You look like an unlikely group to be lawmen."

"We're sorta- kinda like lawmen but we don't have badges."

"Are you bounty hunters, then?" The doctor frowned as his eyes narrowed.

"No, we are *not* bounty hunters. We work for the bank and right now for Sheriff Boon Cassidy."

As soon as we mentioned the sheriff, the doctor frowned. He sucked on a chew and spat into a tin cup.

"Cassidy, you say?" He said it as though it left a sour taste in his mouth. "I hope you know what you're doing. The sheriff has a bad reputation here in town."

"That is Malvo Tanner," Chito-Ochi said.

The doctor's eyes popped wide, and he replied, "Why didn't ya say so? I've heard nothing but good things about Mr. Tanner."

"What can we do for him, Doc? When is he gonna wake up? He looks might pale."

"All we can do is wait, son. He might wake up in an hour and he might stay in a coma for weeks or months. You just never know. If you have something to do, you had best get on with it. Sitting here staring at your friend isn't going to do him any good. He doesn't even know you two are here or where *he* is, for that matter."

"I ain't budging until he wakes up."

The Indian shook his head and stood. He grabbed my arm and urged me on. "Come on, we must let the doctor take care of Malvo now. We might as well go ahead and do our job. I know for a fact that is what Malvo would want. He's always practical like that. If it were me lying there, he wouldn't sit around wasting time. It was the outlaw's fault that he is like he is. I say we get some old-fashioned revenge." He turned his head toward the doctor. "We'll be back in a couple of days, Doctor. If he comes around, tell him we went after the bank robbers on our own. It's time you grew up, Benji. It's time to earn our pay the hard way. How much money do you need, Doc?"

"We can get to that later," Doc Paloma replied. "I believe I can trust Mr. Tanner. You run along now, and I will take care of things here."

After leaving Malvo's horses and saddle in the stables, we rode west. It was getting late, but we had already wasted enough time. Every minute we let pass, the thieves were getting farther away. I guess I was about to grow up real fast. Now I knew we were on the trail of hardened outlaws. Men who didn't think twice when they killed. It would be get them first or die. I wondered if I was up to it. Then again, I felt I had to seek revenge for my friend.

To be honest, I didn't like the odds. We had heard there were four robbers. With one dead, we still had three, and from the looks of things, they were hardened criminals. If they had the grit to drop back and try to bushwhack us, they obviously weren't very afraid.

I wondered what I had gotten myself into, but I knew it was too late to turn back. I pushed the thought from my mind and closed the gap between the Choctaw Indian and me. I intended to stick to him like glue. If not, I may then be the next man down.

I hope I'm ready for what is to come.

the scrubbs gang

"I wonder what happened to Buster," Buck Scrubbs said. "Our brother should have caught up with us by now. I wonder if they caught him. He's never let us down before. It ain't like him to wander off or not say what he says he's gonna do."

"Don't be silly," Wilber spat. "Nobody can catch our older brother. He's too smart for any Mexican lawmen, and the ragtag posse El Paso mighta put together that fast couldn't be worth much. Heck, we don't even know if anybody is chasing us. We didn't steal all that much money."

"All it takes is for the law to get lucky," Larry said, "or maybe he was bitten by a rattlesnake. There're enough nests down by the river."

"In Juarez?" Buck asked. "Don't be silly. I don't see the town constable having the grit to take Buster on. Sheriff Cassidy is too busy to chase us over the border. That's why we didn't hit the big payroll. Then we'd have fifteen or twenty deputized men after us for sure. I doubt we have much more than three thousand dollars in all. Hardly enough to put together an important number of men to take chase. Still, it's a good day's earnings. The sheriff doesn't like crossin' the river anyhow. It's too dangerous for a man with his reputation. I've heard he's killed too many Mexicans."

"For me, that's plenty of money with half the risk," Wilber said. "We could have done worse. I'd say it's closer to four thousand dollars in all. There are a lot of silver coins in there, and they're double eagles and all. That would give us a thousand each. Not bad money for a couple of days' work."

"Yeah, I doubt it's the El Paso sheriff who's nabbed Buster," Buck said. "As I said, he has too many enemies on this side, and it would be too easy to bushwhack and kill him. If there's anybody, it's probably bounty hunters, or maybe he just fell off his horse. Accidents *do* happen, you know."

The four brothers were distraught because the oldest, Buster, hadn't caught up yet. That was a sure sign that something went wrong. He was the gang leader, after all. He had never had any trouble shooting men from afar before then. He was the family marksman who planned the bank robberies and getaways. It was hard for them to believe their older brother fell prey to some poorly trained lawmen. It had to be somebody else. But the question now was who.

"Maybe we should head back to town and find out what happened," Larry said. "He might be in that broken-down jail. I doubt the Mexican sheriff will be up to taking all four of us on. If he's in jail, I reckon we should go break him out. My guess is the Mexicans got lucky and nabbed him."

"Nah, he's not in jail," Jimmy said. "There's no way that old Mexican lawman could outsmart our brother. His two deputies are too scared to get involved with serious outlaws. It must be something else."

"And what if there's law chasin' us right now?" Buck asked. "There must be somebody on our tails, or Buster would have caught up. When I get the feeling somebody's chasin' us, I'm usually right. Mark my words; we best tread with caution."

"It should have been easy enough to shoot 'em while they were crossing the river if somebody did show." Jimmy huffed. "At least to kill one of 'em and wing one or two others. That usually turns posses around quickly enough. How many members would they send if that's what they did?"

"Maybe he just ran out of luck. The only reason I can see that he ain't here is that he's shot or dead." Wilber groaned. "I've got a bad feeling about all this. Maybe we best cut our losses and hightail it out of here before we get caught or killed, too."

"And leave our brother?" Jimmy asked, shocked. "Are you crazy? I'm not going anywhere until I find out what happened to Buster. He's the head of the family. What would he do if it was one of us back there instead of him?"

"He'd probably use his head, not like you,

fool," Buck spat. "Sometimes you're dumber than a dirt clod. We need to calm down and make a plan. Maybe two of us turn back, and one goes on to the hideout with our money to make sure it's hidden before somebody catches up with us. The cash is evidence, and if we don't have it, there's no way they can prove us guilty unless they brought one of those clerks with them, and I believe there's little chance of that. None of them would risk their lives for the bank's money. Especially down here in Mexico."

"Don't look at me like that; I know what you're thinkin'," Wilber replied. "I'm not going to leave my brother back there and run away. He's more important than the money to me. We've always stuck together, haven't we?"

"This isn't the time to bicker," Buck growled. "I'm the number two man in this family, and in Buster's absence, it'll be me that makes the decisions—not you fools. Each one of you is dumber than the other. You're lucky there are some smart men in the Scrubbs family."

Nobody dared talk back to Buck, not because they believed he was any smarter than them, but because he was the meanest member of the family and half again as big as any of them. He eyed one and then the other through squinted eyes.

"Now let me think for a minute so I can devise a plan," Buck said.

He didn't expect any more rebellion from his brothers. Maybe it was time he ran the family and not his big brother. He knew he wasn't as bright, but he believed his brawn made up for it.

"And put that dad-gummed fire out, fools. We don't want to advertise where we are. There aren't that many miles between us and Juarez, ya know. We aren't safe yet by a long shot."

twenty-five
time to grow up

We carefully crawled through the bushes. I was right behind Chito-Ochi. I was so close that I could see the wear on the soles of his moccasins. If I lost my way now, it would probably cost me my life. Lucky for us, one of the outlaws was taken out by Malvo Tanner. Now, it was only four against one. Hopefully, they didn't know we were so close. At least, that was what the Choctaw said. At this point, I didn't know what to believe.

My mind shot back to Malvo. The last we saw of him, he was unconscious on a gurney, and things looked bad. I suddenly realized I didn't have my full attention on the job at hand and knew it was dangerous. I had to force thoughts from my mind and give the situation my full attention. I knew I might not get out of this if I didn't. I may end up like our friend, Tanner. Near-death and maybe dying—if he wasn't already dead.

We traveled silently, so we hadn't spoken a word for hours. There was only the soft sounds of our horses' hooves clopping on dirt and sand. We traveled at a low lope for half a day, then at a fast trot through the afternoon, changing our mounts as needed. It wouldn't do to wear them out too much in case one came up lame or we had to make a run for it. I was as nervous as a cat on a hot tin roof. I had to bite my tongue not to speak.

As the sun set, Chito-Ochi signaled for us to dismount, and we tied our animals back away from where we thought the outlaws lay. I had no idea how the Indian followed the thieves to where we were, but I didn't doubt his skills. If he said they were close by, then I reckoned he was probably right. Who was I to question an expert tracker and warrior, no less? I was just a teenager, but something told me I was about to grow up fast.

I had to remind myself to breathe every little bit. Sweat rolled off my brow into my eyes, making them sting, but I didn't even dare blink in case I missed a vital hand signal from my Indian friend. His mouth was no more than a gash, and his eyes were slits. He reminded me of a giant snake. Somehow, he seemed to be able to see in the dark without making a sound. I followed his tracks precisely so I could move in silence, too.

I felt safer traveling into danger with him than I ever did with Malvo. I wondered why that was. It was something that I felt in my gut more than anything I could figure out with logic. My instinct told me that if I followed him precisely, we might make it out of this alive.

Then again, if Malvo could fall, both of us could, too. I suddenly found myself in more danger than ever

—except when the Comanche attacked our farm. I guess there would never be anything as bad as that, no matter how long I managed to live. Now, I wasn't even sure I would survive the night.

We seemed to crawl for hours, but I knew it had to have been no more than minutes. Still, I struggled through the brambles and briars. Blood ran down my face from scratches when we crawled through thorn bushes. The Choctaw Indian picked an almost impossible route to the outlaws' campsite.

I suddenly realized his thoughts. Nobody would ever expect us to come upon them from here. On the other side was the rock face of a crevasse, so they felt safe in their little cubby hole. It was even difficult to see their fire from afar.

From one moment to the next, we were thrown into darkness. I even heard one of them grumble and say to extinguish the fire. Chito-Ochi looked back at me and pointed to his eyes as he closed his. Somehow, I knew he wanted me to adjust to the total darkness before I opened them again. How I knew this, I had no idea. Was it Indian telepathy? Could this mysterious man send me his thoughts? With a simple gesture, he told me what to do, and I had no doubts.

Focus on your actions, fool, before you get shot, and stop being stupid. Nobody can transmit their thoughts. Think about what you're doing, or you might spend the rest of eternity right here.

Chito-Ochi motioned for me to crawl up beside him. I saw him pull his pistols. Rifles would be worthless at such close quarters. I wondered for a moment if he planned to kill them all. They were responsible for Malvo's condition, even if they weren't the ones who did it. If they hadn't robbed the bank, Tanner wouldn't be lying on a bed, maybe dead.

The thought ran a cold chill up my spine and into my brain—I shuddered. Again, I had to push the dreadful thoughts from my mind and make myself focus on the moment at hand. I could feel the tension increase. Everything was just about to blow up.

The Indian looked at me sternly. His eyes said for me to pull myself together. As soon as I heard him draw back the hammers of his revolvers, I knew things were just about to go to the dogs. Time had just run out, and whatever was coming would happen in the next seconds.

When I saw him jump to his feet, I did the same, despite my dreadful fear. I felt like I was just about to sacrifice my life and all for the whim of an Indian I hardly knew. Then again, with Malvo dead or dying, he might be the only friend I had.

A gunshot sounded out, and a flame flashed in the dark. It was right beside me, and the boom rang in my ears.

"That bullet was a warning shot, but the next ones are for you!" Chito-Ochi yelled. "Drop your guns now or die."

I lay on my belly holding the big Colt Walker, ready to pop off a careful shot like in a dream. Suddenly, the truth settled in, and my eyes spread. For the second time in my life, I was looking death in the eye.

I had the mind to draw my hammers back, too. The

click was much louder than expected. Now they knew we were two, and we had the drop on them. Something moved in the corner of my eye, and before I knew it, I shot the man closest to me. He had a pistol in his hand, and it was pointing my way.

My partner's revolvers roared, too, and another outlaw fell, wriggling in the dirt—two down and two to go. I was surprised how we made such short work of them. The Choctaw's plan had worked perfectly, and it looked like I would live to see another sunrise.

Both men began to cry when they saw their wounded brothers. All the fight seemed to fade away, and they dropped to their knees and bawled like babies. They acted like they didn't even remember we were there. I've never seen anything like it. Right then, I hoped I never did again.

The realization hit me like a locomotive. It took my breath away. I had taken a man's life, and I was so close that even with only the stars to see, I could see the look in his eyes when he felt the hot lead puncture his chest —the accusing look he gave me. I had just taken away everything he had and everything he was ever going to have. I knew as soon as I shot him that he was going to die.

What I hadn't expected was all the screaming and yelling when the shock passed, and the pain hit both mortally wounded outlaws. It shocked me like I never expected. I always knew one day I might be called on to do such a thing—especially riding with Malvo Tanner with his reputation and after the brutal murder of my family back on the ranch.

Like sacrificing an animal, I always believed it would be quick and clean. It wasn't like that at all. The screams seemed to last most of the night. I never imagined killing a man up close would be so noisy and make me so nervous. I was more fraught from the yells of pain than the act itself. It never dawned on me that they wouldn't die immediately. Now, as nervous as I was, I had to watch them suffer until their spirit abandoned their bodies.

Their cries were full of dread, pain, and suffering. Ultimately, like babies, they both called for their mama. I gasped when it ended. Then it was far too silent—almost nerve-rackingly so. The only sound was of the soft weeping of the remaining brothers. They had lost their family in the briefest of moments. I knew precisely how I felt, but they had brought this on themselves, unlike my ma, pa, and James.

Little by little, they became less intense as their energy floundered, and their lives began to slip away. The man Chito-Ochi shot died just after mine. I nearly started crying and probably would have if I had been alone. The fact that I had taken another man's life as I looked right at him rocked me to the core. I had no idea it would be like this. Did this mean I would go to Hell? I certainly hoped not. I believed what we were doing was for the good of man, or at least I hoped and prayed so.

We waited for the morning before we attempted to move, even with only two prisoners. Of course, we were going to take the dead bodies back, to prove we'd done the job. It was as important as the live captives. It was proof that they had not only robbed a bank but caused other men to die for their evil deeds. That weighed heavy in a court of law in Texas.

Everything became visible when the sun rose, and light crept across the land. Blood was everywhere. Somehow, I had it all over my hands and gun. It must have been the spatter from the man I shot. The campsite looked like a butcher shop. I wiped my brow and looked at the back of my hands. They were red with claret.

I sat there in a trance until Chito-Ochi gently touched my shoulder. "We are ready to go now. I saddled the horses and tied the two dead bodies down. Get your horses and prepare to leave. We still must pick up Malvo. I won't leave him here in Mexico. If he dies, I want him to be with his people."

I looked up and saw the last outlaws alive sitting on a single horse with their hands tied behind their backs. Another rope ran under the horse's belly and was tied to their ankles. There was no way Chito-Ochi was going to let these men escape. I could see he was still angry about his partner, Malvo. It was there in his eyes for anyone to see—he was itching to kill them both. Maybe it was my presence that saved the grace of the last villains. Still, I knew as soon as he got back to El Paso, they would hang for what they had done.

It was broad daylight when we rode into the Texas town on the border. Seeing dead men on the backs of horses apparently upset the town's citizens—especially as we hadn't had time to clean ourselves of all the blood and gore. It was like I was in a trance. This might have been the second worst day in my young life. Now, I had graduated to being a killer, and I didn't know how I felt about it. All I knew was I was confused, and I had a bad feeling inside like I'd never had before.

I rode beside Larry Scrubbs and his brother, the sole survivors of their family. Chito-Ochi drove a buck-board wagon, which the doctor loaned us to bring Malvo back home. He still hadn't regained consciousness. By now, I figured he was a goner, too.

It was all I could do to take the prisoners into the jail cell and watch as Boon locked them up. I never felt so exhausted in my entire life.

The sheriff pointed to a bunk in an empty cell and said, "Lay down and take a load off, young man. You look like you've traveled a thousand miles. With a few hours of rest, you'll feel like a new man. Nobody will bother you here. I doubt you prisoners over there will have much to say. They haven't stopped crying since I locked them in their cell."

"In a way, I reckon I have been on a long journey. At least it seems that way." I was still reeling from the killing and our narrow escape. Then, fatigue fell over me like a ton of bricks. My mind numbed and the world went dark.

I was curled up in a ball on the empty cot and, in two minutes, I was snoring softly. I'd never been so tired. Then again, I had never killed anyone that closely, either. I took a lot more out of me than I ever expected.

The main cell block door slammed with a bang, and I even heard the sheriff lock it with a noisy big key. Then, I was off into my dreams. Or were they nightmares? At this point, it was hard to tell. All I wanted then was darkness and for my spinning mind to stop. Right before I fell asleep, I wondered if Malvo would be alive when I woke up. He was right across the street at Doctor Sound's office.

In the haze of my dream, Chito-Ochi and I walked across the street with heavy feet. Putting one foot in front of the other was a monumental effort. When we came to the door, the Indian stopped, closed his eyes, and said a silent prayer to his gods. Hopefully, they would spare the life of a man who had become almost like a brother. When we pushed the door open, all we could hear was silence.

twenty-six
my latin affair

When I woke up the following day, I pushed myself up and onto my elbows. I blinked the sleep from my eyes and saw Boon sitting on a chair outside my open jail cell door. He had his arms crossed with his chin propped up in his hand. His questioning face told the story. He wondered if what I'd done had changed me for the better or for the worse. That was something I still didn't know. I continued, too confused to think straight.

"I have hot coffee on the stove if you fancy," Boon said. "You've been asleep for a day and a half. Chito-Ochi said you killed a man. I remember my first, too. Number one is always the hardest. It gets easier from then on out."

I blinked my eyes in wonder. For a moment, I thought it was all a dream. Then the truth hit me in the face like the hot kiss at the end of a hard fist. I looked down at my hands, and they were black with dried blood. Pieces of flesh speckled my boots.

"I need to wash up. I'm a mess."

"There's a tub around the back. You can take a bath and then wash your clothes. There's a tin of hydrogen peroxide in the cabinet by the door to the yard. It's with the rolls of bandages. That will take most of that blood out of your new duds. There are some old rags there, too. Help yourself."

A large kettle of steaming water sat on the stove. Rather than making coffee, I used it to warm up the water for my much-needed bath. I found a block of lye soap, stripped off my boots, shirt, and britches, and sat back in the warm water to soak. I could feel the tension begin to drift away. I almost got sleepy again, but I had slept enough. I needed to find out what was going on. Had Malvo died, or was he still hanging on by a thread?

That was when I remembered I had promised myself to visit Miranda as soon as I got back. My, how things had changed in the last days. I felt like I was living another life. I shook my head to remove the cobwebs and began to rub the stains on my new clothes. I didn't want to visit my intended girl like I was. Her father would turn me away straight away.

It took two hours to clean myself and my clothing. The South Texan sun dried them out in minutes. I fished in my pocket for a nickel. I planned to have the shoeshine boy by the saloons buff my boots. I brushed the dust off my new white hat. I wanted to look my best. I already knew Miranda enough, but I had never spoken to her father, and I knew he was an important figure in town. I knew I had to make an impression.

When I passed the church, with its high walls and massive doors standing open, I realized it was Sunday. I had lost track of the days of the week. Organ music floated on puffs of air as the parishioners sang with open hymn books, following the words with their fingers. I was almost tempted to go inside. I'd never been in a Catholic Church.

Ranch hands and bosses rode into town—their rifles upright before them, the buttplates on their thighs. A flock of pigeons scattered, bursting into the air, and fled to the ruins of three haciendas at the edge of city. They were from the times of the Spanish and were crumbling into ruins. The church was sullen in the bright sunlight. Town dogs barked somewhere in the distance.

Cats carefully crossed high walls where they were safe. Vultures stood shoulder to shoulder, eating the town's garbage. They lifted one foot, then the other, holding their wings out like open coats. A coyote crouched between its thin legs as it hid, waiting for me to pass. I looked up and studied the naked mountain ranges beyond the horizon.

The outcrops of stone lay in dark tethers of shadows. As I walked down the street, my nervousness increased with every step. I had waited for this moment for days, and now that it was near, I began to feel like I might chicken out.

When I looked at the sun again, I realized it was nearly suppertime. I hoped that I wasn't barging in. All the things that could go wrong began to flow through my head. Suddenly, I realized I was standing on Miranda's porch.

I felt sweat running down my face and wiped it off with my sleeve. I pushed my shirt into my britches and used my handkerchief to polish my new belt buckle. I looked down at my boots, and they shone. I wrapped my hand into a fist and stood poised to knock on the door. Then, out of the corner of my eye, I saw something.

"Whatcha want, boy?" Mr. Frank asked, nearly sending me into a panic.

"I, er, came to see Miss Miranda, sir. I know who you are, Mr. Frank. I work for Malvo Tanner. Maybe you've seen me around."

"I know who you are too, son, although we haven't been properly introduced. Well, go on and knock. There ain't nobody gonna bite ya around here."

"I'm Benji Willow, Mr. Frank. I'm mighty pleased to meet ya."

"You sure do have some fine duds. They look like they just came out of the box," Mr. Frank said. "You go ahead and call me Ben. Any friend of Malvo's is a friend of mine. We've known each other for a long time. The same goes with the Choctaw Indian, Chito-Ochi. I'd be hard pressed to find better men."

I was impressed that Malvo's reputation was so good. I wondered if he knew what happened.

"How is Malvo doin', anyway? I heard he hit his head and is in a coma or somethin'. Is that right?"

"I'm afraid so, sir, and Chito-Ochi seems plenty

worried. I reckon they've been riding together for a long time."

"That they have. Well, with the Good Lord's will, he'll wake up and be as good as new. A man must think positive, or life out here this far west is too hard."

"Yes, sir, I'll try to remember that."

I turned and knocked on the door. When I looked back, I saw that Ben Frank had vanished. I breathed a sigh of relief and thanked him for that. I was more nervous than a rat locked in a cage with a cat. That was when the door opened, and my heart melted.

"It's about time you came by to see me," Miranda said with her fists on her hips. "I was just about to give up on you, Benji Willow."

As she said my name, it made my belly itchy, and it did flip-flops. She made me feel special like nobody had ever done before.

Suddenly, I felt shy. I looked at the toes of my boots. My heart soared when I raised my head and looked into her eyes. I almost melted when she smiled. Right then, I knew she was the girl for me. Now, I had to make myself worthy of such a prize.

"I came over as soon as I got back from Mexico. I came to meet your ma and pa. That and take you for a stroll around town, if that's all right with them. And, of course, with you, Miranda." I liked the way her name rolled off my tongue.

"You better come in first and meet my mother." Miranda huffed. "She's not the piece of cake my father is. Make sure you say ma'am and are all polite, or she might not let us go."

"Don't worry. My ma taught me good manners. She's gonna like me just fine. My pa always said I was a true gentleman, and I reckon he was rarely wrong."

As I expected, the meeting with Missus Frank was smooth sailing. I don't know why, but older women always trusted me and were impressed by my behavior. I kind of thought I swept her off her feet—maybe even more than I did Miranda. I saw I was going to have to work for that.

In no time, we were walking down the street. I stole little glances at her from the side of my eyes. I was shocked when she grabbed my arm and locked hers in mine. It felt so good that I forgot all the bad things that had happened in the last few days. I pushed it back into the corner of my mind and enjoyed the moment I had been waiting for.

"What do you have planned for your life, Mr. Willow?" Miranda asked. "Do you know what you want to do or be?"

"Well, I reckon I already have a pretty good job, that is if my boss recovers. He was injured in the line of duty in Socorro, New Mexico. As soon as he's back on his feet, I reckon we'll all get back to work."

"And who else works with you?"

"Oh, I work with *them*, ma'am. I'm not the boss or anything. Malvo Tanner and Chito-Ochi run the show."

"Why, Malvo is a friend of my father's."

"You don't say? Funny he didn't mention it."

"Don't be surprised. Mr. Tanner is not much of a talker, but his Choctaw friend is nice enough. I don't mean he is mean or anything like that. It's just that he's always so serious."

"Serious? Yeah, I reckon he is a bit, ma'am."

"And stop calling me ma'am. We're the same age, aren't we? You can call me Miranda like all my close friends."

When she mentioned my age, my heart skipped a beat. I really didn't want to tell her. She would think I was just a boy when I hadn't felt like a boy since the Comanche attack. I've even killed a man, although in the line of duty and on the right side of the law. Right then, I felt just about as grown up as I had ever wanted. Maybe even a little more than expected.

"All right, Miranda."

I took a chance and looked deep into her eyes, and I almost got lost for a moment. Then we both grew broad grins and broke into a skip as we made our way across town. I even dared grab her hand, squeezing hers, and she squeezed mine back. That was when she shot me a wicked look, leaving me wondering what it meant.

twenty-seven
deputy willow

I just stood shocked when Chito-Ochi told me the news. My face turned as white as a ghost. I had considered what would happen if Malvo didn't recuperate, but I was still left in a state of disbelief. Everything I had planned for my future suddenly went up in smoke.

"But he isn't dead, is he?"

"No, but he hasn't woken up, either," Chito-Ochi replied. "For now, we must call it quits with the business. A lone Indian can't hunt down White men on his own. I'd end up strung up to a tree, myself. I have some family near San Antonio I haven't seen for a long time. I believe I will visit them for a while. If there are any changes, send me a message on the weekly stage. There's nothing I can do for him here but worry, and that is not my way."

"We did it when we got the bank robbers. It was just you and me."

"Yes, and we were angry and lucky nothing went wrong. You are too young, and I am an Indian. We will have to wait to see what happens to Malvo. Whether he survives or not will decide our future."

"When are you going?"

"The stage is waiting in front of the Wells Fargo station as we speak. They are ready to leave now. Come on, walk with me. We can't make them wait for an Indian. The White people will get angry. I'll ride on top with the shotgun guard, so I don't scare the women. The driver is a friend of Malvo's and mine."

"What am I gonna do? I guess I'm out of a job."

"I have talked to Henry, and you can stay in the stable stall for as long as you want. For now, go see Sheriff Boon Cassidy. He might give you work. He can always use somebody to sweep up. Do you still have any money left from the hundred dollars? With Malvo unconscious, we still have not been paid by the bank. We will have to wait and see what happens. They don't like giving Indians money."

"I still have a lot of money—at least, it's a lot for me. It must be around forty dollars. If we ever get paid for catching the outlaws, there will be that, too. I'll get by until Malvo gets better. You watch how he snaps out of it."

Chito-Ochi nodded and tried to smile, but it was a hollow effort. He saw it in my eyes; I knew it, too. It looked like he didn't expect Malvo Tanner to regain consciousness. It *had* been over a week.

When I visited him this morning, his cheeks were sunken, and his face was pale and lifeless. He looked like a rubber doll. A shudder racked my body, but I did my best to hide it. Still, the Indian saw what was in my thoughts, but there was nothing more to say. That was the way of life lately. It seemed like everything was spinning out of control, and it never seemed to stop.

"Well, you take care of yourself, Chito-Ochi. I'll miss having you around. Yeah, you're probably right. Sheriff Cassidy will probably give me a job. He seemed to have taken a shine to me anyway. Don't worry about me. I'll get by just fine. But before you leave, I want to tell you how much I appreciate all you've done for me. I wouldn't be alive today if it weren't for you and Malvo."

"It was my—er, our pleasure. Malvo took a shining to you right off. To be honest, I never thought he had it in him, but somehow, you brought out the father instinct buried deep inside. I could see it when he looked you in the eyes."

I proffered my hand after I wiped my cheek with the back of my hand. I hope he didn't see the tear, but I had to admit, I was all shaken up.

We shook hands like two old friends, and he turned and climbed aboard the stage, and it instantly jerked into motion. We didn't even have time to wave. I felt my heart sink right then and there. I'd never felt so alone in my entire life. I stood in the middle of the street with my hat in my hands until a wagon roared by, and I had to jump to keep from getting run over. Dust chased the wheels down the street, and I stood to the side, dumbfounded.

As I made my way down the road, I gravitated toward the sheriff's office. I hadn't thought about where I was going, but maybe in my subconscious, I knew that was the only way I had to turn. Before I knew it, I was standing before the El Paso sheriff's office and jailhouse. Maybe Boon would let me stay in a bunk for a while.

I'd been bit to pieces by chiggers sleeping in the horse stall, and the hay made my skin itch. When I looked up at the sign, I got confused again and sat at the end of the porch with my head in my hands. Maybe I wasn't so grown up after all. Right then, I felt as lost as I did when I climbed out of the well to find my family scalped and murdered.

As I lay my forehead in my arms, resting on my knees, I felt the presence of somebody when the wood planks groaned. I looked up and saw Boon sitting beside me. He didn't look me in the face. I reckon he didn't want to embarrass me. He must have known I had been crying.

"Havin' a hard time there, pardner?" Boon smiled. It transformed his face into a kinder man.

"I reckon I am, Sheriff. I just lost my job and my two best friends."

"Why, ain't I your friend, too? Don't be stingy now. How about if I offer you a job?"

I nodded, resigned. I guess I had no choice, but I hated to go from sort of being a law enforcement officer to sweeping up. It looked like I was going to trade my gun for a broom.

Boon looked at me harder than usual. "How about I offer you a job as my new deputy? Lord knows the two I have ain't worth squat. If you are good enough to work with Malvo Tanner, I reckon you're good enough to be my new deputy sheriff."

I blinked. I suddenly realized my mouth was gaping open.

"Be careful, or you're gonna catch a fly." Boon laughed.

I thought fast and lied. "I'm sixteen, just like Miranda Frank."

"Ya don't say. It ain't all that big of a deal. As my deputy, all you'll have to do is watch the town when I must ride out into the county someplace. You won't have to go past the city limits. How about that for work? And I'll pay you a hundred dollars a month. If you're out of money, I'll give it to you in advance."

"No, I have plenty of money—at least for now. But I need a steady job. Since Comanche murdered my folks, I'm sort of on my own. At least, I was until Malvo and Chito-Ochi found me. If they hadn't, I reckon I'd have perished. It's a shame about Mr. Tanner. He saved my life, ya know."

"Well, get your gear from the livery stables. Tonight, you can bunk in an empty cell. That works for me so I can sleep at home for a change. I think it'll work for us both. I've needed somebody reliable for a spell, and you need a job and somewhere to sleep. I reckon your new job can remedy both."

"That's mighty kind of ya, Boon. I don't know what to say."

"Save the thanks for when some outlaw comes to town when I'm away, and you've got to deal with it yourself. That's part of the job, Deputy. Come on in, and let me officially swear you in. I think I have an extra badge for you in my desk drawer somewhere."

When he pinned the badge on my chest, I knew I blushed. How did I go from a kid running from the Comanche to the El Paso, Texas, deputy sheriff? Things were moving so fast my head spun nearly out of control. I wondered what Miranda would think of me now. More importantly, what would her father think? I knew he was the one I had to please first, regardless of what he said about his wife. She had been a piece of cake.

"Let's go make the rounds, Deputy." He pulled a silver-plated pocket watch from his waistcoat pocket. "Maybe we can have something to eat at the Palace Saloon. Strap on your gun belt. You can't walk out into the street like that, unarmed. You're a lawman now, son, and you're gonna have to make the ornery ones respect you right off, or you'll have problems. Life is full of blisters, Benji. But I reckon you already know that."

As soon as we walked into the street, the sun glinted off my new shiny tin badge, making me feel a full foot taller. I puffed out my chest like Boon and tried to copy his swagger. Maybe this was going to work out better than I thought.

Every store we stopped in, Boon introduced me as his new deputy. To be honest, I couldn't have been prouder. It made the ranch boy of a few weeks ago appear to be somebody else entirely. Now, people looked at me like I was a man instead of a boy. Between the new duds and the rumors that got around town about the dead outlaws, people suddenly began to respect me.

I'd always heard that respect was a hard thing to acquire. I apparently had done that and didn't even know how. It was all a mystery to me. I never imagined growing up would be so complicated.

"Are ya hungry?" Boon asked. "As the town law, we get our grub for free. Mind you, I always leave a little tip for the waiter. I figure it's only fair. What do you feel like eating?"

"Why, I always fancy steak if somebody asks. That or pork chops."

"Then, let's go over to Cid's diner. The cook there makes a tasty apple pie. Don't worry; they have the second-best steaks in town. They're much better than the Palace."

I could feel my grin stretch my cheeks.

"And who has the best?"

"We'll save that for tomorrow. One restaurant at a time. Are you a drinking man?"

"No, sir, I'm afraid I'm not."

"That's too bad because I get all the liquor I want for free, too." Boon smiled. "It's one of the perks of the job."

I couldn't help but wonder if the sheriff drank a lot. I remember Malvo disapproving of drinking every day. He said it was something to reserve for celebrations on occasion. I guess everybody was different like that. Then again, I really didn't know Boon all that much yet. Not like I did Malvo and Chito-Ochi.

twenty-eight
defiance

It was strange, but as soon as Sheriff Cassidy rode out of town, I got a bad feeling. It was almost like I knew something terrible was going to happen. I told myself I was being silly, but it was something I couldn't shake. Maybe it was because it was my first time in charge of the town. Heck, I was only fourteen, even if I was tall for my age, and now, I was the only law there was in a place as rough as El Paso.

I watched Boon's horse become a dot on the horizon and then disappear. I turned around and began to walk down the street slowly. To be honest, I hadn't done much more than sweep up around the jail cell, feed the prisoners staying the night to sleep off their whiskey, and eat for free in diners and saloons. Now, it looked like my job just turned serious.

Until now, the fringe benefits were far better than running down outlaws across county lines like I did with Malvo. I wondered if the sheriff was as good a person as Mr. Tanner. At first, I didn't like him much, but later, I thought he seemed to have a soft spot for me in his heart.

So far, Boon seemed like a good person, although I noticed that he drank a lot. Then again, that was a common trait among lawmen in the West as far as I could see. I suppose with such a daunting task, they might need the courage alcohol gave.

I made a beeline for the sheriff's office. When I reached the porch, my boot heels echoed off the wood plank floor. I used my key to open the door and pushed my way inside and over to the gun rack. I grabbed the key in the top drawer as I passed by Boon's desk. The bottom drawer held a bottle of whiskey and a glass. Winchesters, Henry rifles, and two shotguns stood vertically in the rack. A fine chain ran through the trigger guards, keeping them safely out of reach of passing prisoners.

Of course, they were all unloaded. It wouldn't be the first time the sheriff had someone try to pull a gun down on the way to the cell block in the back. Some prisoners couldn't resist the allure and took a chance. They, in turn, received a beating with the barrel of a gun.

Now, it looked like I would have to pay my dues, and I wasn't sure if I was up to it. Sure, I had killed a man, but I had Chito-Ochi by my side telling me precisely what to do. I suddenly realized I was lonely again, and I didn't have the slightest idea of how to act. All I knew was I couldn't let anyone see any weakness. That would certainly bring trouble and quick. This land was littered with hard men, and some could see my actions as a vulnerability.

I grabbed the double-barrel shotgun and a pocketful of shells from a secure cabinet. I broke the breech, dropped two fresh rounds in, and snapped the shotgun closed with the flick of my wrist. I had much more experience with rifles and twelve-gauges than with pistols, so it would be a more appropriate weapon if I did have trouble. Something I really hoped I didn't.

It would allow me to face down multiple men simultaneously. The original barrel had twelve inches removed, making for a wide pattern buckshot. It would make it impossible to miss if I did have to use it. All I had to do was get close enough. It was a heck of a lot more intimidating, too. Men who would stand up to revolvers would usually pass when facing a small cannon.

I spun on my heels, bucking up to the job. It was time to make the noon rounds. I locked the door behind me and slowly walked down Main Street. For some reason, I felt as small as an ant. Even the shotgun felt enormous in my hands. Holding the double-barrel in the crook of my arm, I wiped the white from the edges of my bone-dry mouth with the back of my hand.

I was surprised when couples walked by; the men tipped their hats, and the women batted their eyes. I guessed they were saluting the badge more than anything. Of course, the sheriff knew about the incident in Mexico with Malvo and the Choctaw Indian, but I doubted it was public knowledge. Tanner wasn't the kind of man to appreciate wild rumors, nor did he want anybody snooping around in his business. Since I had never heard him talk about the past, I believed he would rather keep that to himself, too.

Somehow, I now saw the town differently. I hadn't noticed all the shadows in the alleys before, nor had I spotted the people watching from afar. Suddenly, everybody seemed suspect. I admonished myself for going into a mental panic when nothing had happened. I was probably just paranoid because it was my first day alone. When working for Malvo, I never made a move on my own, and everybody knew where we stood.

Since my new boss had yet to outline exactly what I was supposed to do, I followed his daily routine, hoping for the best. All I knew was that I was supposed to keep the peace in a dangerous town. At my age, I doubted it would be an easy task, but I also knew I had to do my best, or I might get fired when Boon returned. Then where would I go?

I found myself wading into something out of my depth. A cat screamed behind me, and I spun on my heels and leveled the shotgun at the feline. I felt my face turn red and looked around to see if anybody saw me. I was embarrassed, and the day had just started. I felt like I was about to jump out of my skin, but I knew if I didn't get a grip on myself, things would go sideways, and the sheriff had just left town.

After carefully walking every street in El Paso, I finally stopped at the Palace Saloon. Music floated out the windows. I pushed through the batwing doors—they closed on springs, whooshing behind me. As I looked around, I realized that nobody even turned their heads my way. It was like I never walked into the tavern.

Without Boon, it appeared that I was just another nobody. The shiny tin star didn't mean anything without a determined man behind it, and I doubted that I was that person. I was still only a boy trying to look like a man.

In the past when I came there with the sheriff, *nobody* ignored *him*. As I made my way to the end of the bar, I suddenly realized how unimportant I was. I leaned my scattergun against the wall, hung my elbows on the bar, and waited for service.

"How about a glass of milk, please?"

The bartender nodded, chuckling. "I've got a fresh pail out back, Deputy. Give me a minute, and I'll be right with you."

He disappeared out the door, and I found myself alone at the bar with three town bullies. Boon had pointed them out to me a few days before. He said they were all hot air but looked ornery enough to me.

When the bartender returned with a pitcher and a mug, the men at the other end of the bar snickered and pointed. I knew I was supposed to act above such behavior, so I tried to ignore them.

I took a long string of gulps, nearly emptied the mug, then grabbed the pitcher and filled it again. I never seemed to get enough milk.

"That's some mighty fine cow juice, Mr. Barns."

"Call me Billy, Deputy. All my friends do."

"Then you can call me Benji. I have few friends, but I'm always looking for more."

He turned his head when the men at the end of the bar made a snide comment, but the barman wasn't there to keep the law. He was a simple man and was only interested in serving coffee and drinks. He looked at me hard, like he was asking me if I would tolerate their behavior. With one look, he didn't give me an option. They were calling me out.

"I reckon I'd better ask for forgiveness for what I'm about to do, Billy. It looks like they won't stop until I make them."

The bartender looked at me, puzzled, like he wasn't sure what I was talking about. When he realized what I meant, it was too late. The blast was deafening. Plaster from the ceiling flew wild. The three men at the other end of the bar dove for cover flat on the floor, but I kept calm and aimed the remaining barrel at them.

"Do you have a problem with me, mister? Or maybe your two friends? I figure if you do, we could settle it right here and now. It appears you don't find my drinking milk so funny now, do ya?"

When they looked down at the black holes of the double-barrel, their knees trembled, and blood drained from their faces. It looked like this wasn't what they expected from me, and that's exactly what I wanted. I moved the gun barrel, motioning for them to get up.

"We don't have any problem with you, Deputy," the leader of the three stuttered. "N-n-no problem at all—I'd be pleased if you'd let us invite you to, ah, drink."

He almost snickered but thought better and shut his mouth like a steel trap. I suddenly realized how scary it must be staring down the barrel of a scattergun from fifteen feet. All three pairs of eyes stayed glued to the weapon in my fists.

"You wouldn't want to make me nervous, would you? If I pulled this trigger, it would probably cut you in half and kill your friends to boot. Don't you think? Maybe it's time you all moseyed on for the day. I don't wanna see you again—until at least tomorrow."

Without another word, they hurried out the door. It whooshed behind them as the wake of dust followed their boot heels. They couldn't get out of the saloon quickly enough.

I held it together until they disappeared, and then I realized I wasn't breathing. I gasped for air as sweat began to pour down my brow. Luckily, I wiped it off before Billy saw how nervous I was. It had been a close call, but I had used my head and bluffed my way out of a clear and present danger. I wondered if I could pull it off again were it was necessary. This job looked like it would be more complicated than I thought, and I had just gotten started.

Billy leaned on the bar like nothing happened and said, "I doubt they'll be back here for a while."

The bartender spat into a mug and shined it with a dirty towel. He appeared to forget what had happened only minutes before. Maybe this was more typical of a normal day's work than I expected. I sure hoped it didn't get worse.

"I'm sorry about the loss of business, Billy. It wasn't my intention, and I'll pay to have the roof replastered. Just let me know how much it costs. I'm afraid it was the only way I could escape without bloodshed. I hope they're scared enough to leave it be. I don't want any trouble."

"Don't mention it, Benji. That was the best fun I've had all month. Those three are a constant pain in my backside. Good riddance to them all. But don't you think you're in the wrong job if you don't want trouble? I figure that's the only kind of work a lawman has in El Paso. The folks in this town ain't daisies."

Somehow, I made it through the day and the next without incident. I was bedding down when I heard someone messing with the lock on the front door. For the previous two days, I hadn't let the scattergun out of my reach. I was constantly looking over my shoulder, expecting the bullies to hit me when I least expected it. Would they be so bold as to break into the jail to get me alone? I wasn't going to take any chances.

I grabbed the shotgun and shifted through the dark shadows near the door. I waited with my thumb on the hammers with the triggers pulled. As soon as I fanned the hammers, whoever was trying to break in would get both barrels. I waited silently as sweat dripped off my chin, making a small puddle beside my new boots. Drops exploded on the floor like tiny bombs.

Lucky for me, Boon had the mind to shout out, "It's me, Sheriff Cassidy," he growled. "Don't shoot, Deputy!"

I could see his teeth when he snarled while walking into the room. He scratched a match on his britches, lit the lamp on his desk, and went straight for the whiskey drawer.

I guess I held my breath so long I began to get dizzy, and then I gasped for air.

"I sure am glad it's you, sir. I thought maybe somebody was trying to break in."

"Were you expecting somebody else?" Boon asked as he filled the glass with liquor and turned it bottoms up. It didn't sound like he was in a good mood. "Who would have the gumption to break into a jail unless they wanted to bust somebody out? Did you have any trouble while I was gone?"

I hesitated momentarily, then answered, "A little with those three bullies you pointed out the other day in the Palace Saloon, but nothing else."

"I've been meaning to set those three straight for a long time. Maybe it's gonna be their lucky night." He downed another glass of whiskey like it was water. "And stop aiming that cannon at me, young man! It's a good way to get yourself killed. If it were anyone else, I'd have shot ya already."

Somehow, I felt he meant it. Boon was obviously drunk and in a bad mood. I hadn't seen him like this before. A man with a badge and a grudge was a dangerous combination. I aimed the shotgun at the floor, but I didn't put it down, and I kept my thumb on a hammer just in case. This didn't seem to be the same sheriff I talked to before he left.

"Is there anything I can do for you before I turn in, Sheriff?"

He didn't answer but instead got up, pushed the chair over with the backs of his legs, and staggered to the door.

I retreated to my bunk in the last cell but kept the shotgun close by. I hardly slept that night as I waited for Boon's return. Maybe the sheriff would be too tired to be ornery, but I didn't want to take any chances. When the roosters crowed their early morning announcements, I still sat in my bunk with the scattergun in my fists. Right then, I figured I had better get a new job. Something told me Sheriff Cassidy was dangerous, especially when he was drunk.

Three days later, I was still trying to figure out how to quit and not anger the sheriff. I realized that I was not in his debt. I struggled along with my hands in my armpits like some thief with something to hide as I frantically walked the streets, wondering what to do next.

I didn't even like being in the sheriff's office with the boss. Three days had passed, and he had been drunk ever since he returned. Something must have happened that ticked him off. That was why I kept the shotgun strapped across my back. I knew I could never outdraw him, but at least with the scattergun, I couldn't miss if I did have the chance to protect myself.

I was sitting on the porch, trying to be as small as possible, when I saw the sheriff stagger radically down the street. When he navigated his way to the porch, he had to use the post to climb up the single step. Even then, he nearly fell.

"What are you doin' out here sitting on your tail?" Boon growled. "Don't you have somethin' to sweep up?"

He staggered to the last cell and dropped

into my bunk. That must have been where he slept off his binges before I came to work as a deputy. It looked like I wouldn't have a place to rest for a while. I planned to stay as far away from him as possible until he sobered up.

Now what? I guess I'll sleep on the porch. At least there, if he shoots me, he will have to do it in public.

Then I heard Boon yell from inside, "Before you fall asleep, go down to the Palace Saloon and bring those three bullies back. You best take a wheelbarrow with ya because I know they can't walk."

A chill ran up my spine when I realized what I had inadvertently done. I had sicced a dangerous man on three buffoons, and now I felt guilty, and I was supposed to be the one keeping the law. I took being a deputy more seriously than Boon did, and he was the sheriff. Or was it all just a façade?

I walked around back and found a wheelbarrow. The rusty axle squeaked all the way down the street. Billy was using a mop to clean up the blood when I pushed my way into the bar. Dark red puddles lay scattered across the floor. In a pile lay the three men who had had a go at me earlier. It didn't look like they would give me more trouble today. Their faces were bloodied and swollen.

"He beat 'em with his pistols, Benji. I ain't ever seen nothin' so fierce. I could have sworn he was gonna kill 'em. Be careful when you go back to the office. The sheriff is in one of his moods again."

One of his moods—again? Is this something that I was going to have to deal with often? My guess was that was why I never saw the other two deputies. They were doing El Paso County law work far from the sheriff, where it was less dangerous. He hired me to work here in town. I remember Boon said I wouldn't have to leave the city limits. I wondered if that was by design or coincidence. Now, I didn't know how to get out of the job. Things were getting dodgier all the time.

twenty-nine
change of air

It was early the next day, and the sheriff still hadn't stirred, and I was sweating bullets. I didn't know where to turn. I could imagine how hungover he was going to be. I tiptoed out onto the porch with my boots in my hands, carefully closing the door behind me. My mind screamed when the wooden planks groaned under my feet, but I looked back, and he didn't stir.

The sheriff continued to snore loudly, then stopped, and I froze. But I didn't hear the bunk springs squeak. Maybe I was safe for now—only time would tell. I was more careful than ever to ensure I didn't make a squeak. I walked in my stocking feet to the end, sitting on the edge and pulling on my boots.

I wondered if this job was worth a hundred dollars a month. At first, it seemed fine, with free food and a place to sleep. Then the sheriff's true nature came out, and I saw I'd made a mistake. It wasn't only me that thought it, either. Apparently, his binges were as regular as clockwork, but this was still the first one *I* had seen.

From what I had heard in the last day, Boon seemed to be drunk often, and when he drank, he got ornery. That was the problem I now faced. My pa always said there was nothing worse than a nasty drunk. It looked like I was about to discover how bad that would be. I had walked right into it with my eyes wide open, and if I didn't tread lightly, they would probably end up black and blue.

Now, the trick would be to get out of this job without getting locked up or shot and, at the same time, maintain my reputation. What I saw in the last few days completely changed my opinion of Sheriff Boon Cassidy. Now, I clearly saw how dangerous he could be, and I wasn't sure that aggression wouldn't turn against me one day.

I had to sleep in the same building, not twenty feet away. He hadn't stopped since he started drinking several days before. I wondered how long it would take or if he'd had enough for now. Eventually, he would probably head back to his house, but when? My evening peace and quiet was lost until he sobered up.

If I quit, where would I go to find a new job? Hanging around with the sheriff probably didn't help my reputation. Some people might get the wrong idea and believe that I was like him when I didn't even drink. Still, I knew that a man had to make his own way this far west. If I didn't have a means to make a living, it was going to get tough and quick.

There were no handouts for drifters and jobless bums. I wondered if I was stuck with what I got and when I had felt so confident working with Malvo and the Choctaw Indian. It was too bad that it had to end, but it was a future that I could no longer count on. I felt that now things were going to be different. Exactly how different, only time would tell.

I didn't know why, but Tanner and Chito-Ochi made me feel welcome and safe—something I hadn't felt since the incident. I could see now that the ship had sailed, though. It had been weeks since the injury, and Tanner showed no signs of recovery. The only bright side was he remained alive—but what kind of life was he living?

Things certainly didn't look promising for his future. To survive only to be a vegetable lying on a cold slab seemed hardly worth it, especially for such an active man. Chito-Ochi never even returned. I believed this said a lot about the situation and our futures.

Had the Choctaw thought Malvo's survival was possible, I believed he would have come back. Now, my only friends had disappeared, and I got caught in a trap like a fly on a sticky strip of honeyed paper. The allure of the money and a steady job made me jump into something without seeing where I would land. My inexperience and young age had gone against me, and I didn't know enough to be able to judge situations clearly.

I didn't know why Chito-Ochi hadn't returned. In such a wild country, anybody could get killed or seriously injured. Maybe it was because he was unable. I'd hate to think he abandoned his friend.

Then again, I had already. I didn't have much experience with Indians and had always heard they had strange ways. Most said they were challenging for White men to understand—especially when the Choctaw appeared and disappeared on a whim. Right then, I couldn't think of anything I would like more than to see him pop up, but there hadn't been another sign, and the country was too big for me to find anybody. I didn't even know how to track.

I finished pulling my boots on and my pants legs down to the crown. I decided to head for the diner and breakfast. My spurs jingled as I shuffled down the road. Free food turned out to be the only good thing about this job. While I still had it, I decided I could take advantage. When I entered the diner, the waiter saw me and scurried over to take my order, but he wasn't his old friendly self. At least he didn't seem to be to me.

When I noticed his nervousness, I figured he was also afraid of Boon. The other times we visited, I hadn't noticed, but now I was looking for hints about my boss's true nature. Did everybody grovel at his feet when he came for whatever he wanted to eat or drink? Was the free food because he refused to pay? Right then, there were too many questions and not enough answers. I felt like I was still in the dark and didn't like where things were going.

What excuse would get me out of my current situation without getting into more trouble and making me look like a fool? If I got a bad name because I walked away from my second job, perhaps nobody else would be interested in hiring me for a third. Was I destined to drive cattle for the rest of my life? It could have been worse.

I could have died back on the Red River with the rest of my family instead of hiding in the well and making my escape. Maybe had I died too, it would have been best for everybody in the end, though—perhaps even me. I didn't seem to have so much to live for after all. Suddenly, I felt terribly alone again, and the cloud's shadow covered me, hanging low.

One way or another, I believed the sheriff ruined my chances of getting a good start in the South Texas town—that, and of course, the accident of my former boss. Maybe my only way forward was to buck up and deal with it like a man. I didn't think he would shoot me like he mentioned. Then again, when a man got as drunk as he did, you just never knew. He was known for his gunfights and apparently never lost. I imagined that, for some of them, he might have been drunk, too.

I kicked a can down the dusty street, thinking about my labyrinth of problems. Every way I looked at it, I saw a dead end. In the time since the murders and the farmhouse got burned on the Red River, I had already run through two employments, and I was only fourteen years old. I was beginning to think I wouldn't make it to fifteen.

I was all up to wearing a star. I thought it would make me respected. Everything was great initially, but the newness began to fade quickly. Now, all I wanted to do was get it off my chest, but I feared it would be more difficult than expected. If I ever got another chance, I planned to look hard at my path before walking because the next step may be to my grave.

It dawned on me that maybe I'd shot myself in the

foot and now had no future in this part of the country. From what I heard, people knew the sheriff far and wide, and much of that gossip wasn't very good. But where would I go then if I left El Paso? I knew how dangerous it was in town, but how difficult would it be out in the country, especially as a young man alone?

This question weighed heavy on my mind. I needed to figure out where to look from here. I had no intention of asking to return to live with my relatives back East. I didn't know if they would have me after so many years. I wasn't the young boy they knew when I left. That was almost six years ago.

Now that I thought about it, I would hate to try to make the journey back up the Chisholm Trail again—especially on my own. It goes right past the Red River, where I buried my folks. Here, I thought my bad streak of luck had ended when it appeared to have just begun.

thirty
different times

The next day, I sat on the porch, fretting about my current situation. The more I thought about it, the more trouble I felt I was in. I made a big mistake taking the job as deputy, and now I would have to suffer the consequences of my error of judgment. Then again, what choice did I have? Nobody else was ready to take an *orphan* in, much less give me a job.

I thanked my lucky stars; I looked older than I was. Only Malvo and Chito-Ochi knew the truth. I had told them my real age but would lie from then on. Nobody was going to trust a young kid. I didn't have the shadow of a beard.

When I said the word orphan, it stuck in my mind. It was the first time I'd let it sink in. I was so busy surviving that I had thought little about anything but getting to the next day alive. I just realized I had joined the rank of waifs. All I could do now was try to avoid becoming a ragamuffin.

At this point, the only option left open for me was

to work as a cowboy on a ranch or cattle herd. The way things were currently, I felt that anything would be better than where I was. Still, it was one thing to own a ranch and another to give your life away for a hundred dollars a month, twenty-four hours a day, seven days a week, riding line or drag.

I believed it had to be dangerous in the Texan countryside, from outlaws as much as hostile Indians. Everywhere I'd seen since leaving the Red River was more dangerous than the previous place, and El Paso topped them all. Now, I was looking at another hurdle, and if I wasn't careful, it could cost me my life.

As a gloomy mood fell over me, I sat on the porch all morning, staring into the distance. I had already made the morning rounds first thing, and after the commotion from the sheriff the day before, nobody was stepping out of line.

Three bullies lay battered in one of the cells. Two had bunks, and the other slept off the beating on the hard adobe floor. As soon as they were released, I knew they would go and hole up at their ranch, an hour from town. It would give them time to lick their wounds, but I doubted they would forget what happened and who was responsible. They wouldn't be brave enough to take on the sheriff, but they probably believed I would be an easy target.

Something told me I had not seen the last of those three. I didn't know their names, but I believed they would remember mine. They didn't seem like the forgiving kind. The sheriff probably told them why he came, too.

I sent him there, but I had no idea he would go so far. I had made myself three enemies, and one day, we would meet again. One against three was no deadfall, even if I had my guns. Every day, things seemed to become more complicated.

I wondered how many adversaries the sheriff had. By the way he acted while drinking, I imagined he had plenty. I didn't mind admitting it to Billy, the bartender. I told him the sheriff scared me just as much as he did him, but he told me he had seen much worse, which made me even more concerned. Instead of heading to the cell for the night to sleep it off, others were sent directly to Boot Hill and an unmarked grave.

I fingered the scattergun in my hands. I hadn't been out of my reach since the sheriff started drinking and had no plans to put it away anytime soon. If forced, it could be a deterrent if Boon got aggressive with *me* like he did with those in Palace Saloon. I never imagined he could be such a mean piece of work.

Then again, it took a hard man to do what was necessary to keep the peace in such a lawless land like Texas. Nobody seemed to understand anything but violence. And here I sat in El Paso, still the deputy. I found myself in a complicated situation.

Behind me, I heard somebody hack and spit; then boot heels crossed the inside of the room. I knew who it was without looking, but still, I didn't turn. When the screen door suddenly banged shut, I nearly jumped an inch off the porch. As I sat with my back to Boon, I frowned but knew I had to turn around. When I did, I gave him the best smile I could muster. I knew I had to make the best of things because I knew no other way to survive.

"Good morning, boss. How are you feeling today? It's a mighty fine day."

Surprising me, Boon replied, smiling, "I feel like a million dollars. I guess I worked all the meanness out. I need to do that occasionally, or it gets all built up inside, and I get into a dark mood."

If he was in a dark mood when he didn't drink, I couldn't imagine how mean this man could become while inebriated. I guessed the rumors I'd heard about the killings were true, after all. Some said it was a dozen, and others even more. Until then, I thought it was more gossip than truth, but it dawned on me that much of what I heard now made sense.

"There's hot coffee on the stove, Sheriff. Give me a few minutes, and I'll make us some frying pan biscuits and bacon."

"Thank ya kindly, boy, but a cup of java will suit me for now." Boon nodded.

Sheriff Cassidy slapped his hands on his chest and smiled, ducking back inside for his first coffee of the day. I was surprised; he seemed in a better mood than I had expected. Yet, I knew behind that façade of calm lay a dangerous gunfighter.

When I turned back to the street, I had to rub my eyes to ensure I wasn't seeing things. Chito-Ochi was walking two horses my way. A smile grew wide across his face, making his brow wrinkle and dimples appear. After weeks away, I assumed that the Indian would never return. I had stopped checking in on Malvo seven days ago. I didn't have the heart to see a man so full of life lay there and wither away.

It made me feel guilty, but I had so much on my plate that I didn't know which way to turn. The disappointment I felt each time I saw Tanner lying there brought the whole incident back to me like it happened yesterday. I just couldn't watch him die.

Despite my worry, I suddenly found myself so happy that my stomach felt all bubbly inside. I never thought I would be so glad to see an Indian. Chito-Ochi wasn't an average man, though. He was unlike any I'd ever met. Just seeing him made me feel safer again. I didn't know why, but it did.

"Benji Willow!" The Choctaw Indian smiled. "It's good to see you are still alive. I, too, have been fortunate; the spirits have looked down on me with goodwill, and I have survived. Are you ready?"

"Whatcha mean, am I ready? What are you doing here? I thought you'd never come back. Have you heard something that I haven't?"

"I'm going to see Malvo. He talked to me in a dream. He said if I came and gave him a fresh breath of life, he would return to the world of the living and leave death behind."

Even though I didn't believe in Indian spirits, I still hoped the Choctaw's words held some truth. Yet, I had been to see Malvo only a week before, and there was no change at all at the time. Doc Adam Sound said the only change he noticed was losing too much weight. He talked like he had little hope of Malvo's survival. Maybe that was why *I* gave up hope. I should have known better about that, too. It appeared I still had a lot to learn.

Chito-Ochi claimed he had talked to a man who had been unconscious for weeks. I wanted to believe him with all my heart, but my skepticism kept me from doing so. I was a White boy, and he was an Indian, after all.

The Choctaw Indian stopped before the jailhouse porch and asked, "What are you waiting for? I came to get you first. I knew you would want to come along. If I'm not mistaken, our friend will be waiting for us to arrive."

"But what about my job as deputy?"

"I'm sure Boon will understand. Once Malvo is back on his feet, he can speak with him. If the sheriff respects or fears anyone, it would be Tanner."

"You seem awfully sure of yourself. How do you know he's going to get better? He didn't look very good to me the last time I saw him. Maybe my faith isn't as deep as yours; then again, I'm not Choctaw."

As we neared the doctor's office, my feet became heavier with each step. I wanted Chito-Ochi to be correct, but I knew he had to be wrong. When we reached the door, I knocked, and my Indian friend shook his head.

"We can walk in; you don't need to knock. He doesn't know we're coming, but he'll be awake now. Like I told you, he spoke to me in my dream. I doubt he knows I heard him, but we *are* like brothers. If I remember correctly, you had a twin. Then you probably know what I mean. It's no small thing being so close to someone."

I pushed the door in, not at all convinced. I saw movement in the back corner as soon as our eyes adjusted to the light. My eyes must have grown the size of saucers. Maybe there was more to this Indian than I had thought, yet my mind told me it was just a coincidence. Still, I was happy with the outcome anyway. Malvo was sitting up in bed with a cup of soup in his steady hands. His face was pale, but the forever-determined look was back in his eyes.

"Is that you, Malvo?" I couldn't believe what I saw. He was sitting up, sipping on a bowl. "When did you wake up?"

"Why, just this morning. I was wondering if you would come, Chito-Ochi. I saw you in a dream. I heard you were working with Boon Cassidy, Benji. We'll have to put an end to that. I can't let a man like him take away one of my men."

The Choctaw Indian smiled and said, "That is why I came. So, we would all be together again."

It almost felt like I was seeing my old family, even though we weren't related.

"You can't believe how happy I am to see you survived, Malvo. It's like a miracle, and not a small one at that."

"It doesn't seem like such a big deal to me," Malvo replied. "Other than feeling tired, I would have thought I only went to sleep yesterday—what day is it? How many days have I been out? Did we get the outlaws? The last thing I remember was when I was about to fall off my horse and at a bad time. How did all that pan out?"

"We took care of everything just as planned, but they still haven't paid us since you were unconscious. They said they couldn't give bounty money to an Indian or a boy. I figures it was just an excuse. Now, they will have to give us what's ours."

"What? Don't worry, boys; nobody's going to get away without paying *me*. You still need to tell me. How many days was I out? I feel like it was only hours."

"It wasn't like you think," Chito-Ochi replied. "It was more like several weeks. I believe you are blessed by White men's spirits and Choctaw gods. You are a fortunate man, Malvo Tanner. Not everyone can say they came back from the dead."

At that point, I didn't know what to think and didn't care why Malvo got better. All that mattered to me was that he was alive, and things were going to go back to the way they were—at least, I hoped so.

thirty-one
recovery

We moved Malvo out of the doctor's recovery ward the following day. He was the patient who had spent the longest time there without dying. Doc Sound rented him a large room in one of his buildings. The town doctor didn't drink, had no vices, and used his money wisely. As a favor to Malvo, he leased the place with three beds for eight dollars a month. In a couple of days, it felt like home. It was a darned sight better than the sheriff's jail cell bunk.

With each passing day, Tanner seemed to grow stronger. Chito-Ochi often fed him strange-smelling concoctions, and despite the foul taste, it seemed to quicken his recovery. I saw the look on Malvo's face every time he had to pinch his nose and swallow. In only a few days, he was up and walking around town several times a day, exercising weakened muscles. Chito-Ochi and I always accompanied him. Tanner claimed he felt the same as always, and the doctor disregarded brain damage. It looked like he would be his old self in no time.

We were all aware that he had the most enemies of the three of us, although we all had a few. I had three but doubted if they bothered me now that Tanner was up and around. That alone gave me peace of mind. He was a perfect example of a man whose reputation preceded him. He was different from the sheriff because he did good things for others and not bad. Sure, he, too, had killed men, but most of them needed it, and others were in self-defense. He was there to defend the defenseless, and Chito-Ochi and I were his helpers.

Sometimes, I wondered at night how all this came about. There was no apparent rhyme or reason for how things happened. Still, Chito-Ochi claimed it was all decided many winters ago—something I didn't understand. Malvo wouldn't give me an opinion on something he found too silly to waste his time thinking about. Still, like most young men, I wanted to know how the world worked and every nut and bolt in it. My curiosity asked me why things were like they were and where I would go in the future, even though most questions were unanswerable.

"How about something to eat?" Malvo asked. "Where do you boys wanna go? It's my treat for making you wait for me all these weeks. For me, it seemed like a couple of hours."

"Let's go eat at the Palace Restaurant. I've made friends with Billy, the bartender. He always keeps a quarter pail of milk set aside for me. I want to tell him

I've got my old job back. He doesn't like Sheriff Cassidy, either."

"As far as I'm concerned, you never lost it, son," Malvo said, smiling. "Your job, I mean. You jumped to conclusions and acted rashly. It would have helped if you had waited patiently like Chito-Ochi, and he should have known better than to tell you to go to Boon for a job. Still, he did the smart thing and spent the time visiting his family."

Tanner rubbed my head, rustling my hair like a little boy. I didn't know if he noticed me turn red or not. Then again, in a way, I didn't mind. I could use a couple of good friends right now. Strangely enough, one was an Indian, something I hadn't seen coming. It turned out that Chito-Ochi might be more honorable than them all. Me? I still didn't know precisely who I was or what I would do, and I believed I might take some time to figure it all out. Hopefully, I would make better decisions in the future, but for now it had worked out fine.

a look at:
Stagecoach (Benjie Willow the Orphan Series 2)

Kidnapped allies. A stagecoach ambush. And a boy too stubborn to quit...

Fourteen-year-old Benjie Willow is barely catching his breath after surviving the Red River massacre. Now recovering in El Paso alongside the grizzled frontiersman Malvo Tanner and the quiet Choctaw scout Chito-Oche, he's finally found a glimmer of stability—until the frontier snatches it away again.

When the trio signs on as guards for a Butterfield Overland Stage hauling silver through outlaw country, they know the risks. But nothing prepares Benjie for the ambush that follows —gunfire in the dust, comrades captured, and a bounty on their heads.

Benjie is the only one left free. And he's the only one who knows what really happened.

Now, with nothing but his instincts, a borrowed rifle, and a fierce determination not to lose the only family he has left, Benjie must grow up fast. In a world where coming-of-age means life or death, he's about to learn what it truly costs to stand alone.

Will Benjie outwit the men who took everything—or die trying to get it back?

AVAILABLE SEPTEMBER 2025

about the author

Born in 1886 in Southern Ohio, Ash Lingam grew crops, raised cattle, and doted on the young boy. Ash's family was among the early settlers in pre-Revolutionary America. He has traced his lineage back to around 1746 when his ancestors immigrated from Europe to the aspiring American Colonies.

A retired marketing executive, Ash devotes his spare time to training police dogs and writing novels. He has found his niche in the Western, historical fiction, and adventure genres. With his vast vault of experience, he never runs out of sources for new stories. He has lived in eleven different countries and worked in a total of forty-six to date, Ash has written approximately 130 novels, short stories, and poems. More than one hundred of his eclectic titles help the American frontier come alive for his readers.

https://www.ashlingam.com/